Sweet Sexy Sadie
McKenna Clan Series Book Two

Christine Young

Chapter One

Princess...

Brody prowled through the boulders and sparse timber. Heat from the sun warmed the earth. He'd just finished his daily run and was about to shift back to his human form when he caught sight of the sexy lady in short shorts. He lifted his head and sniffed, smelling the wind and finding the heady scent of lemon in the air.

My God! The sight of the girl sent shock waves reverberating through him. Tremors swept through his body, his heart lurching then stopping for a split second.

Brody needed to see this lady close up. He'd had dreams about her—he just didn't know who she was or what she was going to be to him. And he'd never clearly seen her face. He was about to do just that. He'd never thought he would meet the woman he'd been dreaming about. And there she was, standing beside her overheated 1990's mustang.

His heart screamed at him. His senses whirled on overload and every nerve ending felt as if it snapped. Currents of electricity jolted through him in a tat-tat-tat machine gun blast. The sensations were even more intense than when he shifted to his jaguar form. He found his clothes then changed into human form, hopping on one foot as he tried to get both feet into his jeans. Then jumping as if that movement would help the zipper close.

Wiping sweat from his brow then checking to see if he'd fastened his pants, he sauntered toward the girl who had let her car overheat in the desert. He wasn't quite sure what he was going to say, but he'd figure that out as soon as possible. Nice to meet you seemed boring.

A good pick up line here would be nice. Every rational and coherent thought vanished from his head. Numb and empty, he stood behind her and rocked back on his heels. Sweat beaded on his forehead then trickled down the side of his face. He couldn't take his eyes off her cute little butt, which was sticking up in the air as she seemed to study the engine of her car. When she shifted feet and her rear swayed from one side to the other, he knew he needed to put his hands there, on her hips and oh so gorgeous curves.

Princess...

"Uhh..." he began.

She jumped. "Oh!" Then turned and her smile melted his once jaded heart. Damn and double damn. This was all good, so good. And she was real good.

"Need some help?" Brody asked as he pointed to the car and the sizzling engine that appeared to need water. Lord, but he needed some of that H_2O stuff. His parched mouth cried out for help and liquid. All his smooth evaporated.

She kicked the tire with a flip-flop clad foot. "I need this piece of junk to run and it doesn't want to." Flipping her hair to the side, she looked back at the object of her wrath and obvious frustration.

"Let me see." He walked to the front of the car and peered inside. If anything, he was trying to give himself time to think of something intelligent to say. At the moment, the thoughts forming in his mind would send her running in the opposite direction. Hot, carnal sex, naked flesh against naked flesh... Too hot, too soon. Do you want to fuck? Hell, where was his head?

"Looks like your radiator overheated."

"Tell me something I don't know. The steam is hotter than the Sierra Madres sun." She pushed the wisp of red hair that had escaped her ponytail behind her ear and looked skyward. "Does it ever rain around here? No, don't answer that. I'm sure once a year liquid comes from the sky and it's not going to be today."

He grinned then leaned on the car, arms crossed in front of him. "Got a bottle of water in there?"

"No."

"You come into the desert without water?" Disbelief as well as denial that someone would drive through the desert without water swept within. "Did you think there are rest stops every twenty miles?" He heard the puff of air she let out and wanted to laugh.

"I'm only ten minutes from town." Indignation laced her tone.

"You weren't ten minutes an hour ago." The need to protect and let her know about her foolishness overcame good sense. He'd just met her, and she didn't know who he was. He could be Jack the Ripper for all she knew—well, maybe his counterpart. It's all good, he reminded himself. She was fine. No harm, no foul. But what if...

"I drank the water a little ways back. Where's your water and why are you on foot?" she shot back.

"Guess we have to walk to town." Brody stuffed his hands in his pockets, not wanting to answer her question yet.

"Don't you have a cell?"

"Don't take it with me when I run." He shrugged. She looked horrified.

"You run in this heat?"

"Guess I'm used to it. Don't you have a cell?"

"Yeah, but I don't know who to call." She reached inside the car and pulled out a large bag then dug around in it for what seemed an eternity. She paused then and looked at him. "What's your name? I'm Sadie Monroe."

"Brody McKenna. What are you doing in these parts?"

"Research." She shrugged then waved a hand in front of her face.

"That's interesting. Can't find the phone? Want me to look for it?" He'd like nothing more than to get inside her purse, her head and...her gorgeous body. And he'd like to know what she'd be researching in these parts. Not much to study besides cactus, and that seemed a bit ridiculous.

"Here it is." She proudly held the phone up, a beautiful smile gracing her face. "I knew it was in there somewhere."

Dear lord, but he loved her freckles, her hair, her long legs and everything about her. This isn't real, yet he held out his hand for the phone. "I'll call my little bro. He'll be more than happy to come get us before we dehydrate from this searing heat. And he will be more than happy to give a lecture on the practice of driving around here without an ample supply of water."

"There's more than one of you?" she asked, cocking her head a bit sideways and looking at him as she meant to discover all of his secrets.

He'd like that but in reverse. He wanted to learn everything there was to learn about Sadie Monroe. "Yup." He was proud of his brothers and sisters. They were good people, honest and fair, sometimes to a fault. He enjoyed teasing them too. But they always reciprocated.

"A man of few words, I see." She walked down the road a bit, her hand shielding her eyes from the glare of the sun. Then she returned. Her t-shirt molded to her breasts, outlining her curves.

He waited to see what she was up to and when she walked back, he said. "Yup. Just to change your opinion of me though. I have three little brothers and one set of twin sisters."

"Oh..."

Brody punched in his brother's number then waited a second before lifting the phone to his ear.

"Hey, Carr." Brody listened for a while, nodding his head. "Can you come pick Sadie and me up? Sadie's having car trouble and we need a ride. You can send a tow truck too. We're about ten minutes north of town on the old highway. Okay, see ya." Brody handed the phone back to Sadie.

"Your brother's name is Car?" she asked. "That's unusual."

"Mom and Dad decided to give him a Scottish name. It's really Cathair but we call him Carr for short." Brody turned his attention to the boulders across the road. A strange feeling of cold passed through him then vanished. He felt as if someone was out there watching them.

She nodded as if processing the information. Then she asked, "Ok, is your name Scottish too?"

"Native American, and Brody is a nickname. My real name is Bodaway. It means fire maker. Parents must have had a vision because I'm an explosives expert. Love making those big explosions—love the noise and the fire."

She blinked a couple of times. "Don't know what my name means."

"Princess," he told her quickly. "And, you remind me of one, a princess. First time I saw you that's exactly what I thought." His heart raced and his breathing quickened until he felt the need to put his hand over his chest.

She laughed and he liked the sound of her laughter. It was a deep belly laugh and authentic. He wanted to make her laugh all of the time. Needed to hold and protect her. But first he had to find a way to figure out why he had this crazy and a bit insane infatuation with a lady he'd known for just minutes.

At a loss for words, he focused his attention on the road. It would be some time before his brother would arrive. Carr would have to finish whatever he was doing, and he'd have to get the tow truck and set up all of the gear. Then it would take the ten minutes from town that was left. Perhaps it would have been faster to walk.

"We should find some shade." He could have made it easily. But when he'd seen the little flip-flops Sadie wore, he knew walking was not plausible.

"Fine, is there any? Shade?" She had turned in a three hundred sixty degree circle, searching for something there was very little of.

"Under the cactus over there. We could take turns," he told her. "We might find a slip of shade, but at this time of day..."

"How about in my car," she said but didn't seem too excited about the prospect. "At least the seats are more comfortable than hard ground.

So they sat inside the mustang with the doors open to let in the nonexistent breeze. Minutes ticked into an hour before the sound of another car reverberated in the air. A few seconds later, a tow truck appeared around a bend in the road. It rumbled forward at a turtle's pace and painted in big red letters it said, Cactus Junction Towing.

Brody had never been happier to see Carr and the tow truck. He had wanted to ask so many questions he'd had to bite his tongue every few seconds. He didn't want to seem over exuberant or prying. And he was hungry. His brother had arrived just in time to stop him from further making a fool of himself.

"So, where are you staying when you get into town?" Brody hoped it was at the hotel his family owned. He could set her up and see her.

"I have reservations at the hotel."

"The McKenna hotel?" He wanted to invite her to stay with him or at least in his parents' home but knew once again if he did, he was moving too fast too soon. And the last thing he needed was to scare her off. He wiped his brow with the back of his hand. Yeah, his eagerness terrified him.

"Yes," she paused as if putting two and two together. "Your family owns it? Is it nice?"

"Nice enough; we don't get a lot of visitors out here. Mostly miners and sometimes a tourist or two. It's comfortable."

"And researchers," she said with a lift of a perfectly shaped brow.

"You'll be cozy and the food is good."

~ * ~

Sadie didn't know what to make of Brody. Exceptionally handsome and charismatic, he'd made her smile the first time she saw him sauntering down the road toward her. Good lord, but he looked as if he owned the world. Tall, tanned from the sun, amber-green eyes that sparkled as if he saw some light humor in everything. He was wiry and sleek; a quickness about him surprised her. His blue-black hair was tied back with a leather thong, his chin angular.

Perhaps he did own this part of the Sierra Madres. His family seemed to own most of this town.

Her research had brought her to this place, Cactus Junction. Now the prospect of getting to know an interesting man would be an added perk. In the bathroom she slipped out of her clothes and into a tepid shower. A few minutes later she emerged squeaky clean and ready for the next part of her adventure.

Unpacking her clothes and taking out her laptop, she opened it. *What do explosive experts do? Hmmm....*

Why, they blow up things. What would he blow up around here?

Lord but that sounded crazy to her. Before typing in the necessary info to pull something up on Google, she leaned back, relaxing into her chair. The wallpaper was outdated, and the old fan complimented the air conditioning. She realized she liked the atmosphere.

Enough musing. Mining in the Sierra Madres. Let's see, it says here they mined silver as early as 1521.

Sadie scrolled down the paper. Ok... Montezuma, in 1492, was already drinking hot chocolate from goblets made of gold. Maybe she should be studying this instead of her research thesis. The migration of butterflies. Once she'd thought the topic was romantic. Chasing after butterflies...

So what are they doing now? Junior drilling companies... She wondered if that was what the McKenna Clan was, a junior company. How soon was too soon to ask? Probably not on their first dinner together. Knowledge brought power and she firmly believed everything happened for a reason. Then her chance encounter in this place was not a coincidence.

This says the companies are drilling to find the ore. So... Do they still need explosives? If not, he didn't do much for his day job. Perhaps the family had millions stashed away. At first glance this hotel was theirs and Brody had told her the land this town sat on belonged to them. But millions in the Caymans? Probably not.

She closed her laptop. Then leaning back, she shut her eyes and tried to cleanse her mind of all thought. A little catnap might be in order, but her heartbeat so fast she didn't think sleeping was a plausible scenario. Eager to meet the McKenna Clan and begin her research, her body was wound tight as a rubber band ready to snap.

The bag of chips in her purse seemed to call to her just after her stomach growled its discontent. Trying to ignore the excessive calories and her empty belly, she rose and wandered to the window. Dinner would be that much better if she waited. Outside, the sun still beat down and one could see heat waves decorate the street.

The air conditioner chose that moment to blow out cold air. Sadie wrapped her arms around herself then turned the monitor down a notch.

Back at the window she looked at the street below. A man walked down the sidewalk, and as he grew closer, he stopped and shielded his eyes then gazed up to her room. Sadie's breath caught in the back of her throat and another chill swept through her. This time it wasn't caused by the air conditioner. The sight of the man sent an eerie feeling to the pit of her stomach. She stepped back in an attempt to remove herself from his line of sight.

The knock startled her away from the window. She jumped, afraid it might be the man she'd just seen but knowing it wasn't.

"Sadie? Sadie, you in there?" Brody called from outside the door. Damn, but she'd recognize his voice anywhere. A smile crossed her face. She meant to forget the stranger.

"Come in." Sadie looked back to the street below. No one was there. Once again she rubbed her arms. She felt as if a ghost had just swept through her, leaving her cold from her core outward.

"You okay?" Brody stepped inside, looking concerned.

"No, I don't think so. I…" Pausing, she hesitated to tell him what had just happened. What she'd felt. He'd think she was crazy.

"You look as if you saw a ghost." Brody stepped beside her, his hand on her shoulder. "You're white as a sheet." He pulled open the lace window curtain and peered at the street below. Muscles rippled beneath his black t-shirt.

Warmth filled her at his touch, and strangely she felt protected. "I just might have," she murmured as she looked back toward the window. "Do you see anything? I thought..."

"Nothin' down there," he said. "What did you see? It clearly frightened you."

He turned her then so she was looking at his face, his eyes seeming to bore into her soul. "Can you read minds?" Her breath rushed out and her pulse beat a terror filled staccato. "It's as if you know what I'm thinking."

"Tell me what happened." His voice was filled with concern. He seemed to understand her fear. "What you saw."

"Nothing really. I was, well I was just looking out the window and I saw..." Once again she turned to the window not wanting to see the stranger.

"What did you see, Sadie?"

The command in his voice seemed out of place to her, but for some reason she didn't mind. At the moment, it felt good to know someone might have her back. It had been so long since she'd felt close to anyone let alone a man.

She shook her head and stepped back a little. Distance was something she needed at the moment. Thinking clearly took on new meaning when it came to Brody McKenna, and she couldn't fathom why.

"Just a man," she told him. "Just an old man in tattered, ragged clothing." When she spoke those words, it was clear to her why the sight had chills shimmering through her.

"What did he look like?" Brody asked. "I know everyone in this town. Cascade Junction's not that big, two hundred fifty-two residents with one more on the way." His voice was low and raspy as if he was angry at something or someone. But that couldn't be right. He wasn't angry with her.

"He was small, short. His beard was ragged and unkempt, just like the rest of him. He held a hand to his eyes and stared up here. At first I thought he was looking at me as if he could see inside my mind." Now Brody was going to tell her just how stupid she was.

Then his breath hissed inward. "If you ever see that man again or have the feelings you just told me about, I want you to run to me or any of my family who are closest. Don't look back, run." His voice intense and strained caught in his throat.

"You're scaring me. Brody, I don't know your family, just you and Carr." She inhaled a long deep breath, smelling his spicy masculine scent. The process calmed her somewhat.

"I don't mean to, but you need to be wary of your feelings. Sierra Madre is steeped in culture, strange myths and folklore going back centuries and there are things…" Brody gazed out the window as his voice trailed off. He turned back to her, a grim look on his face, creases marring his forehead.

"Things…" she parroted. "What things?" She was a research anthropologist. And she could believe in things, but she liked the tangible. She wanted to see it and feel it and know it existed.

"Let's talk about it later when I'm sure of what you felt and saw. I'll ask my father if he knows anyone matching the description you just gave me." He strode to the door, resting his hand on the knob.

"You're ignoring me or placating me and I don't like it," she told him.

"Listen, I promise we'll talk about it. I want you to know…" He ran his hand through his long silky looking dark hair. "If I must, I think what you saw might be a—you're going to think I'm crazy."

She laughed, "I thought you were going to think I was crazy. Okay, okay, I know I interrupted. What is it?"

"A…" He paused again. His look was one of grave distress. "Chullachaqui. It's a legendary devil of the Peruvian and Brazilian Amazonian jungle. There has been talk of the displacement of one of these possibly two…"

"There are more than one?"

"My brother, Carr, was told by an elder that one was spotted in the hills behind town. They are dangerous, and they are known to lure people to them by disguising themselves as someone you know."

"Oh…"

"You don't believe me."

"No, strangely I do. But it sounds a bit scary. So if I see you, you might not be you. You might be one of these devils. You could be one right now. How would I know?" she asked, taking a step backwards.

"How do you feel about me?" He seemed patient, caring, as if he truly wanted her to understand.

"I think you are the same person I met this afternoon on the highway. The same man who found me the ride into town."

"You need to go with the feeling in your gut. Here," he ran his hand over his stomach. "Remember how you feel when you're around me. You won't have those same feelings with a Chullachaqui. When one is around, I am told, bones feel like ice, and fear is the most prevalent sensation."

She nodded several times. "That's how I felt when that stranger was looking up here. And, I felt violated."

"Then you will know the difference between the devil and me."

"Oh, but I'm wondering if there isn't a bit of the devil in you too," she told him, feeling suddenly more lighthearted than she had several minutes ago.

"Of course there is a bit of the rogue in me. But I'm not evil."

His tone was so serious she wasn't sure if she'd spoken out of turn. "I'm hungry." She picked up her bag then slung it over her

12

shoulder, wishing her last statement would vanish.

"Good, let's go to the Red Neck Watering Hole Bar and Grill." Brody opened the door and gestured for her to go first.

She laughed. "Is that really the bar's name?"

"What better name. This here part of the country is filled with red necks and it is a waterin' hole. Not too many of them in this neck of the woods."

"Is the food good?"

"The best," he said as she accepted his arm and they left her room.

Sadie noted he'd made sure to check the lock on the door.

Inside the bar and grill, laughter and voices reverberated around the room. The scent of hamburgers and fries floated through the air. Sadie's stomach growled.

"Brody, what's up," a friend called out.

Sadie knew what he really meant was who's the new chick. Brody nodded and grinned at the man then ignored him.

"There's a nice corner table." He pointed then placed his hand at the small of her back to guide her in that direction.

"That's not very friendly," she tried gauging his reaction.

"Let's just say I don't want to share you today." He looked at her and winked, his grin charmed the socks off her.

The gesture set a wave of belly laughter through her. "I'd like to meet your friends." She shot him what she hoped was a sexy smile then waved to his acquaintances.

A man stepped from around the corner of the booth they headed for. "You going to introduce this sweet looking woman?"

Chapter Two

"Don't want to." Brody frowned hard, wishing the man, his brother, to disappear. He wasn't about to share Sadie with anyone.

"Hey, big bro," Carr pulled up a chair with a devilish nonchalance. "Don't mind if I join you." He grinned and helped himself to chips and salsa.

"Three is a crowd, Carr." Brody let out a low and what he hoped was a muffled growl. He meant to threaten his brother. Carr should know how he felt about this woman. Too bad he wasn't positive yet, but what he did know was that Sadie was damn important to him.

Carr was taller than his older brother by about two inches and more muscled. His eyes were the same amber green. Anyone looking at them would know they were brothers. But Carr was more playful and carefree. Brody always attributed that to the younger brother syndrome. The oldest always carried more responsibilities on their shoulders. And he was the alpha male in his clan. Was destined to lead. Since he'd met Sadie, though, he'd felt the weight of the world somewhat lifted from his shoulders.

"Hey," Carr motioned to a waitress, "a beer." Then to Brody, "Can't get rid of me that easy." He winked at Sadie then grinned at his big brother, knowing he irritated Brody. "You planin' on hookin' up with this wise guy?"

The waitress nodded then left with a chuckle. Brody was sure she laughed at Carr.

"Thanks for the lift into town today," Sadie said, directing her attention to Carr. "I really do appreciate it even if Brody doesn't seem to agree. I'd be happy to have you eat with us." She cocked her head to one side then slanted Brody a smile that seemed to say she was in control. And it was too soon for her to be alone with him.

Brody settled back into his seat, crossing his arms over his chest, frowning. He studied his brother and Sadie, letting what wasn't said just now sink into his hard skull. The waitress came with all of the drinks. After setting them on the table, the server shot Carr a sexy smile.

"I accept your invitation," Carr said. "Even though Brody doesn't appreciate me as much as you seem to understand me. What are you doing in these parts any way?"

"Working on my thesis. I'm looking for a place my team can set up camp. Have to write a proposal for a grant so I need to find out as much as I can about the area and its people."

"Okay, what is there to research in the Sierra Madres? Just cactus and sand and a few rocky cliffs."

"Let's talk about you." Sadie changed the subject. "Don't feel much like talking shop right now."

Brody growled low in his throat, disliking the fact that Carr seemed to be monopolizing Sadie's time and conversation. He didn't know how, but his little bro would pay for this.

"Nothing to elaborate about me," Carr popped another chip in his mouth. "Work all day, play all night. Don't take anything too seriously. Still livin' at home with my sisters, baby bro and this guy."

"Really," Sadie sipped her beer. "That's interesting."

"We all live at home, all of the family." He couldn't figure out how to rid himself of his little brother. Carr wasn't taking the not so subtle hints he tossed his way.

"Brody said you heard talk about a Chullachaqui in the area." Sadie tapped her fingers on the beer glass in front of her.

"How about it? Have you?" His gaze and all of his attention focused on Carr. He needed to see his brother's expression and gauge what was not said as well as what Carr did say.

Carr coughed on the chip he was in the process of eating then drowned the cough with a long drink. His usual playful grin vanished for an instant. But that was long enough for Brody to note the change.

"So, it's true," Brody sat up straight. He hadn't been sure if the story had been fabricated to keep the kids inside the town's city limits, instead of wandering the hills or if someone really did encounter one of these Amazonian devils.

Carr nodded and the following pause was long and a bit eerie. Brody tried to read Carr's mind, and it seemed Carr tried to telegraph him information without speaking out loud.

Brody felt a sizzle of anger and the tingle of caution ripple down his spine. He looked at Sadie for a moment. Concern for her safety suddenly paramount. He didn't know how much roaming the outskirts of town she planned on doing. But he decided she wasn't going to do anything alone.

"Sadie thinks she might have seen one," Brody needed to make sure Carr understood the danger to her and what it would mean if this demon caught her unprotected. Without supernatural powers, she was too vulnerable by far.

"When was that?" Carr sat up straight, a fire burning in his eyes and a growl forming in his throat.

"This afternoon," Sadie told him, rubbing her arms and shivering. "I've never felt so cold in my entire life. And I've been in

16

some pretty freezing places. The incident, it creeped me out."

Brody drummed fingers on the tabletop as he searched the room. He didn't like the sensations he suddenly had. Someone watched them, but everything in the restaurant seemed normal. Yet he had the feeling Sadie was pulling back, distancing herself from him and the possible time she meant to spend in the area. Carr, along with talk of the Chullachaqui, seemed to give her a reason to direct her attention away from him.

His inner cat gave a low growl then started to prowl through his mind. He'd wanted this first mini date with her to be one where he could get to know her better. Instead, his brother intruded, and now thoughts of an Amazonia devil continued to be in the forefront of their conversation. He knew she was frightened, as well she should be.

He watched as Sadie rubbed her arms and her face grew pale. Once again he searched the room for a clue. Nothing. But wasn't he the one who told her a Chullachaqui was capable of disguising himself as anyone and could take on the form of any animal? There was nothing preordained about their prey. They took anyone they could. No one wanted to be in their line of sight when they needed another human. Brody didn't understand the reasons they sought out humans. All he knew was that they did.

He'd also told her of the cold feeling that would rip through her. Silently, he cursed. He couldn't see anything abnormal in this room, but he'd swear she felt the devil's presence.

"You okay?" Brody reached his hand out to her, wanting to hold on to her and reassure.

"Just…just have those chills I told you about earlier." She looked around the bar. "Can we leave?"

"I'll get take out," he told her then looked at Carr, a grim feeling in his heart. "I'm glad you are here. Stay, and when I get back with the food, I want you to walk with us back to the hotel."

A few minutes later Brody stood in front of the table and extended a hand to help her up. "Ready?" He tried to reassure her with a smile but he didn't think it helped.

Sadie accepted the polite gesture and slipped from the booth. "Ready as I'll ever be."

To Brody, Sadie looked over-the-top nervous. Her eyes, at one point, had glazed a bit. At least she appeared coherent. "Look, we don't know anything for sure. This could all be a hoax. I just want to be extra careful. If there is one, I've got this uncanny feeling he wants you—probably because you are the weakest link in these parts."

Her voice shook, "The weakest link, that's nice to know. Once I had a stalker after me, an internet stalker. Could we just be making more of this than we should? It's a story, folklore. Why do you even believe this creature exists?"

"I'd like to tell you yes, and that the Chullachaqui is just a tale made up to scare the hell out of kids sitting around a campfire in the middle of the night. But I've lived in these hills all my life. And I know there are unexplainable things. Things we don't want to acknowledge exist but they do." *Yes, and what would she think if she discovered my second shape was one of a black jaguar*? He wasn't doing a very good job reassuring her. He scrubbed some lose strands of his hair back with his hands.

Brody handed the package of food to Carr. "Let's walk." He held her hand in his and squeezed gently. "Tell me about this stalker." He swallowed hard and thought about the obvious repercussions as well as the not so obvious ones. He'd kill anyone who harmed her.

She pressed her lips together then inhaled a long deep breath as if searching for courage. "It was just on the internet. He followed everything I did, everything I posted or tweeted."

18

"You had to know him, didn't you?" Carr asked as he walked a few paces behind the couple.

"I didn't, though. He hacked all my files then made comments on my blog and everything I posted. He followed me everywhere online. I changed my passwords a bazillion times, but he found me no matter what I used. Now I have passwords I can't even remember."

"I suppose if he could follow you through cyberspace, he could find you for real," Carr said.

She laughed but it wasn't carefree. "I started up north, chasing the birds and the butterflies and recording their migration down the contiguous states. I've talked to as many people as I could find. I've been in plain sight. I'm pretty easy to locate."

Brody opened the door to the hotel. Silence greeted them as they walked up the stairs to Sadie's room. Once inside, Brody set the places then they sat down to eat their take home dinner.

"I'd like you to meet our great grandfather. He lives about thirty miles out of town," Brody said as he stared out the window. Dusk was falling and pretty soon the full moon would hang thoughtfully in the twilight.

"Yeah, can you ride, cause you're not driving out there. No road, not even a dirt one," Carr added his thoughts. "It's a long hard trip."

"Uh…no, I've never had the privilege of learning." Sadie glanced from one brother to the other then stopped at Brody. "You up for teaching a beginner?"

"It's a two day ride from where we can leave the car and horse trailer. We will stop often and it shouldn't be too taxing on you or the horses. I'll give you the sweetest little filly in the stable."

"Through grueling hills and rocky ravines," Carr graced Sadie with a skeptical look, wiping away any reassurance Brody had just given.

"We'd have to sleep in the open?" Sadie looked skeptical.

"You not okay with that? Actually there is a cave about half way to gramp's home where we can stay the night."

"A cave…I guess I've been reduced to one-liners. Sounds like fun. I may be a newbie where it comes to horseback riding, but I've done my share of time under the stars." She shot Brody a grin that melted his insides. "I'm always up for a new adventure."

"Good, then we will leave tomorrow afternoon. I plan on riding at night and sleeping during the day."

"The heat?" Sadie peered out the window. "It was pretty hot when we were waiting for Carr to pick us up."

"Yeah, probably be more comfortable and the full moon, a Comanche moon, will give us enough light to see by."

"And you're not worried about the dreaded Chullachaqui sneaking up on us." Sadie laughed and to Brody the sound was coupled with a tinge of fear.

"No, I'm not worried," he tried for encouragement and prayed his own trepidation would fail to show. "If he only had to think about himself, he wouldn't worry. But now he had Sadie's safety at the forefront of his mind. He thought about asking Carr or his sister Lyn to ride shotgun but nixed the idea.

"Want me to come with you? I could have your back," Carr pointed out with as easy grin.

"Not this time, little bro." He wanted to tell him three's a crowd again but decided against it. "And it's time for you to leave."

"So soon." Once again Carr winked at Sadie. "Be careful of that one. He's pretty darn tricky. Knows how to sweet talk a girl into his bed."

Brody stood, pushing his chair back with his legs. At his brother's words, a moment of anger flared then evaporated. "I'll call you if I need anything." Carr seemed to enjoy this far too much. But he was right. Carr could have his back. But Brody didn't think he needed it. And he damn well knew he didn't want it.

"I'm sure you won't." Carr sauntered toward the door. Before he left, he turned and once again winked at Sadie.

Brody watched his brother leave then peered out the window before pulling the shade down.

"I don't want you looking out that window tonight—for any reason. Whatever might compel you there, ignore the feeling." The moment he spoke, he knew he could have tempered the command.

Sadie closed her eyes then opened them. Her hand rested on her chest above her heart. "You're scaring me, and that 's not too hard to do right now."

"I don't mean to. But it's better to err on the side of caution, don't you think? Here, let me see your cell phone." Brody picked up Sadie's bag then handed it to her.

She rummaged through it for a few seconds before finding the phone and giving it to him.

Brody punched in his number. Passing it back to her, "Call me anytime tonight. If you hear anything, if you just want to talk, I don't care. Call me."

"You sure?" Her hand shook as she accepted the phone from Brody.

"Absolutely," he paused then stepping beside her, he traced the line of her jaw with his fingertip. Bending close to her ear, he whispered, "I've got this overpowering one of a kind desire to kiss you. May I?"

Her eyebrows rose, but she nodded.

"Good," he said. "I've needed to do this since I saw you bending over your poor dehydrated mustang."

His finger under her chin, he slowly lifted it so she looked into his eyes. Hers were a gorgeous shade of summer sky blue. She blinked as he lowered his mouth to her lips. They were soft and he touched them lightly with his then he ran his tongue across them.

"You taste damn good, princess. Will you open for me?" He so needed to take this kiss one step farther. His hands rested on the small of her back. With a hint of pressure, she moved closer to him. He wondered if she felt his cock, hard, hot and ready for more than he meant to claim tonight.

Sadie didn't say anything but her mouth opened. God, but her taste was so heady as he explored the inside of her mouth. Teeth, tongue, lips; everything to taste left him breathless with longing. Hanging on to this moment paramount in his head, he met her tongue with his own, danced and played with it until he heard a feminine moan of pleasure. Every masculine part of him wanted to pump his fist with the knowledge he'd just won this round, but he didn't want to let go of her.

Moving closer to him, her hands resting on his shoulders, she ran her fingers through his hair. The leather thong he'd bound his hair with fell to the floor. Suddenly, Sadie became the aggressor, the leader in the sexual game they played. She pulled him closer and tasted him. Her tongue ran across his teeth then into his mouth. He growled with the pure sensations coursing through him. And like an inferno he thought he might truly explode from the pleasure. Deep in his throat he let out a low growl. Then slowly pushed her away.

When she looked at him, her eyes were slightly glazed and her lips were moist, swollen slightly form his kisses. With his thumb he stroked her lips and she sucked it into her mouth.

Dear Lord, give me strength.

"I think you are going to need your sleep," Brody watched her breasts and she inhaled long breaths of air as if that tiny kiss had left her winded. He delighted in their sweet movement and could hardly wait to see her naked. Later.

"Are you telling me to stop?" she asked, a purely devilish expression gracing her angelic features. "What if I don't want to?"

"Believe me, I don't want you to stop, but we have a long trip tomorrow and you will need your sleep."

"If I'm to keep up with you." She breathed in a long sigh.

"If you are going to learn to ride a horse."

"All right then."

"Now go to bed and call me if you need anything." He slowly backed away from her and toward the door.

~ * ~

With her hands clasped prayer fashion beneath her chin, Sadie watched Brody saunter from her arms and her room. The quiet snick of the door shutting behind him left her feeling abandoned and alone. She'd never liked those feelings. But ever since she'd left home for college, that's how she'd felt. Perhaps skipping her senior year of high school had not been socially wise. Eager and intellectually ready for college, she said goodbye to dear old dad and left never to return. Her non-existent family life was not something she liked to remember. The memories of her mother leaving her never to return were still painful.

In the bathroom, Sadie took a quick shower and brushed her teeth. Mulling over the days events left her a bit breathless and out of sorts. Nervous energy bounced through her, and she wasn't quite sure if she'd be able to fall asleep. The bed just didn't seem that inviting.

She grimaced then pulled the covers back, slipping into bed then shutting off the light. Staring at the flowered wallpaper did not help her settle into dreamland.

Startled by something, Sadie jumped to a sitting position. The clock on her bed stand read four AM. Hands shaking, she pushed her hair from her face. Scratching noises outside her door left her heart in a frenzied pace. Watching the door as if it would spring open at any moment, she made her way to her cell phone Brody had left on the table then called him.

Please don't be asleep. Please pick up. I'm sorry...It's so late.

A phone rang outside her door just as she heard "Hello" on the other end.

"Brody? Is that you?"

"Yeah, it's all good," he said.

"What?" she blinked quickly as she made her way to the door. Then she pressed an ear on the wood, trying to hear outside in the hallway.

"I'm behind your closed door. Sadie, let me in please."

Still with shaking hands, she touched the chain lock and hesitated. "How do I know it's you?"

"Are you cold?"

"N-no...I'm actually quite hot." She pressed her hands to her burning cheeks then wiped her sweaty palms on her pjs.

"Then I can't be the Chullachaqui," he said with a hint of laughter. "An Amazonian devil would never make you hot."

Quickly, she unlocked the door then opened it, falling into his arms as he entered. "You had me terrified. What happened? I thought I heard a loud...but I was asleep and something woke me up."

"Everything okay?" Carr asked from the hallway as he poked his head around the side of the door.

"Carr?" Sadie squeaked. *What on earth is going on?* "Is everyone in this town outside my door?"

"Go home," Brody told his brother. "I'll take it from here."

"Sit." Sadie's temper kicked into second gear. She didn't really like all this subterfuge. He could have told her what he meant to do. Stand guard duty outside her door. She might have slept better if she'd known.

Brody grinned then obliged her, pulling out a chair then straddling it with his arms resting on the back. "Now what? You look like a baby cat with her claws out and you want to scratch something."

"Tell me why you were outside my door in the middle of the night instead of home in bed."

Brody shrugged. "Wanted to be in your bed."

"The truth, Brody. Now." *Everything happens for a reason...*

"Guard duty. The noise, well, I fell asleep with the chair rocked back on two legs. Carr kicked the legs out when he showed up to take over. That's the reason you woke up. My apologies."

"So what's the plan now? You sent Carr away."

"It's almost morning. Thought I would borrow a pillow and a blanket." His gaze focused on the over stuffed chair near her bed. "If that's okay."

Sadie tossed him what he needed then sat on the bed and watched as he struggled into the chair. He'd set his feet on the table, and he looked entirely uncomfortable.

"There is room on the bed...if you want." Her words were a bit hesitant but seemed to take on momentum as she spoke.

"Too dangerous," he murmured, crossing his arms over his chest and closing his eyes.

Sadie sighed then settled into the bed, pulling up the covers.

From the side of her bed, she heard the creaks and groans of the chair as he moved trying to get comfortable.

"We are adults. We can share a bed," she said as she lined pillows up lengthwise to protect herself from unwanted advances.

"Doubt it, but if you insist."

He rose and a few seconds later he was in her bed. She felt the heat through the sheets, felt desire raw and primal rise from her core. Sleep was not inevitable or perhaps it was exaggerated. Shifting in the bed beside her, Brody didn't seem to be able to find sleep either.

Counting flowers on the wallpaper, easier than sheep, she snuggled in against something warm. Sunlight filtered through the cracks between the window and the shade. At peace with herself was something she didn't remember feeling--ever. But she felt it now.

Then she realized she was spooned up tight against Brody's muscled abs and body. One of his hands encircled her breast and one leg was thrown over her. She felt as one with the world. She should be shocked, should push him away. But truth be told, she wanted this closeness to go on forever.

For a few minutes she rested, absorbing his heat into her and listening to the pounding of her heart. Or was it his? Maybe the beats had melded together to become one.

She felt the kisses across her shoulder, butterfly soft, tender but intoxicating too. Pushing back against him, it was her silent way of applauding his attentions and asking for more. One of his fingers traced her nipple then squeezed and tugged. She couldn't keep a tiny moan of desire from slipping through her lips. Dear God, but this was heaven.

With his mouth, he traced his way up her neck and to her ear, alternating nips and kisses. Against her skin his tongue felt raspy, rough, and it tantalized every part of her then heated to a mercuric level.

Voluntary or involuntary, she didn't know, but she turned in his arms, realizing he'd removed his jeans and shirt sometime while she'd slept. Her skimpy shorty pjs did little to protect. They revealed and tempted.

"Sweet, sexy Sadie," he whispered in her ear then his tongue whirled inside, delightfully tracing the lobe.

She thought she'd just jumped from her skin. Her hands roughed through his soft and oh so sleek hair then down his back to his muscled tight butt. She pulled him to her, reveling in the feel of his hard cock nestled on her belly. She didn't want to think about tomorrow or right from wrong. She just wanted Brody McKenna.

He spread her legs and settled between them. Kissing his way from her ear to her mouth then down her neck, he finally settled on her nipples. With teeth, lips, and tongue he paid homage to each one. Her body ignited and she arched her back as if she could summon more from him. He bit and kissed each one then ran his tongue around her nipple.

One hand slid down her belly then to her clit. He worked his magic, touching her as her walls clenched and tightened then wept for more.

"You have so much cream. I want to taste you. But not yet," he told her through tender kisses.

"Please," was all she could manage to say.

"You don't have to beg," he continued, gently biting then sucking a nipple deep into his mouth, one finger still massaging her clit then moving inside.

Heat roared through her head. She suddenly bucked and moaned, the climax building as he pulled back gazing into her eyes.

"Brody," she called out his name.

"Keep your eyes open, honey. I want to watch when you climax."

She slid over the hill, sensations matching no others she had ever felt. She moved with his rhythm, a beat as old as the mountains and as primal as time. When her body finally stopped bucking and shuddering, he grinned at her. "You are beautiful and the sheen on your body is gorgeous. I want to lick every part of you."

"My heart still races." She could barely breathe.

He set the palm of his hand above her heart. "I feel it and the racing of your breaths. You will calm soon."

~ * ~

Long after Brody and Sadie left the Red Neck Bar and Grill, Akando watched the door, hoping Sadie would return without her man candy. He knew men like Brody McKenna, and he realized getting his woman away from the shapeshifter would not be easy. Ambushing her or luring her would be the only way, and he'd have to be smart. A chance encounter would be plausible.

"Don't tell me you're thinking about that little red-head." Celinda purred in a throaty voice next to the Chullachaqui's ear then ran her tongue around the shell. "I'm tellin' you she' not worth the time or the effort."

"What of it?" He brushed her hand off his shoulder and moved away, not wanting to deal with her advances.

"You shouldn't be so obsessed with the woman. She'll end up being the death of you. I'm warning you..."

"I've wanted her since the first time I saw her in Peru." He remembered that moment.

She was on an expedition of some sort. There were five in her team, and he'd tried to get her away from them. Failed and tried again.

There hadn't been enough time. While he laid plans, they'd packed up camp and left. He made up his mind that he'd find her. She would be his.

"That was several years ago. I can't believe you've stalked her this long."

"Let's go back to our room." Akando needed some time to think and plan.

We could," she licked her lips. "I know a way to get the little tramp off your mind." She pressed in against him and beneath the table she rubbed her hand up his leg.

"I don't want you tonight. I'm going for a walk." He rose and chugged what was left of his beer. Without looking back, the Amazonian devil strode from the bar and onto the sidewalk.

For a moment he paused, looking toward her hotel room. Thoughts of going there and knocking on her door filled his head. He inhaled, catching the scent of sage and cactus.

His gut and his cock tightened as his thoughts revolved around Sadie.

Seconds later Celinda stood by his side. "You can't get rid of me that easily." Her fingers slipped down the front of his pants. She wound her hand around him and squeezed. "See, I can make you feel better even if I can't get the slut out of your head. Come on, fuck me, I dare you." She squeezed again.

He groaned, trying to fight the needs of his body. But Celinda knew what she was doing. He wanted to take her right here in the street. He bent his head and his lips found hers. His tongue darted inside her mouth as his hand closed over her breast. He pushed her into an ally. The darkness covered them. Silence surrounded.

With no hesitation, her skirt was up, her panties off and he was inside her grinding. "Sadie..."

"Bastard." But she moaned when she climaxed. He covered her mouth to keep the noise of her cries at bay. A moment later he'd zipped his pants.

"Go on, I'll follow you later." Sex with Celinda made him want Sadie more. When he closed his eyes, he imagined Sadie naked.

Before she left for the city, he'd have her or die trying.

Chapter Three

Sadie walked from the bathroom, towel drying her hair. The smile she graced Brody with sent his heart into a tailspin. He didn't think he could ever get enough of her. Wrapping his arms around her and keeping her close was all he thought about. She was in his soul. He marveled at how fast his feelings had escalated.

"Hungry?" He tried to distract himself from what he really had on his mind—her naked body next to his, his cock deep inside her walls. Her scent, God but she always smelled like lemons.

"Famished," she popped a strawberry into her mouth then wiped a bit of the juice on the napkin in front of her. "Where did you get this feast?"

He shrugged and pushed more food her way. "I called the restaurant. Sit down and eat. You are going to need nourishment for what I have planned."

The bread still steamed. Sadie broke off a chunk then sat down as she munched on the food. "What do you have scheduled? I should think it might involve meeting your family, besides Carr of course."

Sunlight streamed into the room through almost closed blinds. This morning, Brody had opened them in hopes of making the room a bit more cheery.

He lifted one eyebrow before he leaned toward her and kissed her forehead. "Eat first. We don't have time to go out to the ranch, the family home, but I promise that when we get back from gramp's place, I'll take you to meet everyone."

"I'm warning you. I don't like surprises. Everything has to be in order, in its right and proper place," she shot back to him. "It's such a beautiful day. I want to get outside and bask in the sunshine."

"You'll love this plan and you'll get a chance for the sun to kiss your face." He sat back in his chair, crossing his arms on his chest, his gaze riveted on her, thinking more than the sun would kiss her today.

"Don't you need to eat?"

"Ate while you were in the shower. A waste of time though." Brody wasn't hungry for food. He needed Sadie.

"My shower?"

"Yes," he laughed. "Part of the surprise." He watched her as she nibbled on the food, focusing on her lips then the sway of her breast beneath the terry robe she wore. He wasn't at all sure if he could wait for her to finish eating. Control was underrated. Even though, before Sadie, he'd prided himself on that very facet of his personality.

"That was good," she said as she sipped a cup of coffee and played with the lace doily on the table. "Breakfast…strawberries, hot bread, coffee, you can read my mind."

"No, it's what I like."

He stood and held out his hand. She placed hers in his. It looked so tiny resting on his palm. Bringing her fingers to his lips, he kissed each one, gently sucking them one at a time into his mouth. Her trembling delighted him. She was ready for more sensual play. He wanted her hot and willing for him. He needed her mind on him, on how his lips and tongue felt against her body. Then she would discover the full enchantment of their lovemaking. The scent of lemon and the

32

softness of her skin intoxicated him.

His only question was could he wait?

He had too take his time with her. She followed him to the bed. *Do you want to fuck?*

Didn't sound appropriate at the moment. "Where to start… hmmm…" He placed a gentle kiss behind her ear.

Brody pulled her down beside him. She sat in front of him, her back against his chest. He pushed her hair aside as he trailed kisses across her neck and down the column of her spine.

"Again?" she asked, her breath a puffy little sigh. She scooted against him, finding a perfect place.

"Always." He purred while his hands found the tie on her robe and opened the clothing until he found silken flesh beneath. His fingers settled on her belly as his tongue roamed across her shoulders. "You always taste so good—hot and sweet."

Her head fell back, giving him more opportunities for exploration. Just above the cloth of her robe he could see her nipples. He touched the tip of each one then traced the aureole. "So hot," Sadie murmured. "So frickin' hot." She squirmed as if trying to get closer.

"Sweet, sexy, girl. You're going to be hotter before I'm finished, princess." He kissed across her shoulder while his fingers roamed over her breasts.

"Promise?"

He didn't answer instead Brody turned her. She straddled him, her core open to his questing fingers. But it wasn't his fingers he wanted inside her. It was his tongue. He needed to taste all of her, every portion he could find. His desire so overwhelming, he could barely hold back.

The curls at the apex of her thighs were creamy and white. She was wet for him, needing him, ready for sex. Fascination with her and with her body left him panting with need. His fingers curled and uncurled, needing to mark her as his. But that was way too soon. She was not his, not yet. And he could wait until she was all his.

"I think you should take everything off," he murmured as his tongue found a nipple and he sucked it into his mouth then bit gently. "I might rip something if I try."

"So should you," she told him. "I want to see all of you."

Her hands were settled at his waist such a short distance from his pulsing cock. But if he let her touch him…

Once again it seemed to Brody she meant to take control. She followed his actions with parallel ones. Taking his nipple into her mouth, she bit and laved and teased until he groaned with pure sexual delight.

"Ah, princess… It's so, so good, so sweet, just like you."

Quickly, he turned her. She lay beneath him, her legs spread wide her long red hair in beautiful disarray around her head. He ran his fingers through its length. Then traced her lips with one finger.

"I want…"

"Princess, I think I know what you need."

A second later he had kissed his way to her clit. He laved her with his tongue, tantalized, stroked and teased. Then with his tongue he delved inside her core, felt her walls clench, sucked and nibbled at the apex of her most heated sex, laving the cream.

Her fingers wove into his hair, and with each movement of his tongue, she bucked against him, pulling on his hair. He tasted her cream, felt the sheen of sweat on her beautiful ivory flesh. She moaned and climaxed, shuddering, and he needed to send her to that heaven again and again.

He counted two climaxes then he kissed his way up her belly to her breasts then her mouth. She opened for him, and he explored while his fingers drove inside her tight sheath, sending her to a third pinnacle.

Slowly he brought her down, calming her, soothing her until her heartbeat as well as her breath was a slow steady cadence.

"I don't think I can move," she said.

He pushed her hair from her face then kissed the tip of her nose. "That's why I'm going to let you sleep a little while."

"What about you?"

"Have to get us ready for our trip into the mountains."

"No, I mean…"

She looked as if she didn't know what to say. And he was sure she was thinking about his sexual needs, but she was going to have to say it. "Mean?"

She huffed and he almost laughed.

"Your cock, you…well we didn't… Don't you want to…you are making this difficult. Don't you want release?"

"Of course. Don't have a condom."

"You had time to order breakfast. It seems if you wanted, you could have bought a condom."

"When we have sex, it will be all the better for the wait."

"You really mean that, don't you?" she ran one finger across his jawline then down his neck and across his collarbone. He shuddered. She could do that to him with the softest touch.

Strangely, he did want to wait, but he'd never before postponed his own sexual release. He'd always taken what was offered then left. "For me it will be heavenly bliss. Well, that sounded strange even for me."

She cocked her head slightly, a cat smile on her face. "I will wait with baited breath."

"Good, you won't have long to wait." He rose from the bed and pulled the covers over her. Then he went to the shade and made sure it was pulled tight as well as the curtains. "Sleep, I will be back in about six hours with provisions and clothing suitable for our travel plans. Then we will have dinner and be on our way." He had purpose now and a plan.

"Don't you need to sleep?" Sadie patted the bed beside her. "I'd like to curl up next to you."

"Not the way I'm feeling. I'd be inside you in a blink, condom or not." He looked at his jeans where his stiff cock was pressing against the zipper. Humor was the only way to survive this. He only hoped his need for her would die down a bit while they rode. He couldn't imagine the long ride in this condition.

Brody slipped from the room. Carr was already outside the door for guard duty. His grin told Brody he knew what they'd been sharing. And the glare Brody shot his little brother kept any ensuing comments at bay.

"I'm off to see our sisters for riding boots and jackets. After everything is ready, I'll be back for Sadie. Make sure no one gets in this room."

~ * ~

"Sadie you up?"

Sadie inhaled a long deep breath, trying to calm her jumbled emotions. She'd been in a dizzy since he backed from the room several hours ago. Trying to sleep had been a ridiculous waste of energy. When she closed her eyes, she felt Brody's touch, imagined him inside her.

"Yes, come on in." She opened the door to see the two outrageously tall and handsome brothers standing in the hallway. "My, you two are quite the sight. Don't think I've ever seen two such striking men together.

"Everything packed up?"

"Again, yes. I'm not understanding why though." Sadie motioned to the men. Her one large suitcase as well as her backpack sat near the door. Can I take my laptop?"

Brody shook his head. "Any recording of data you do will have to be done the old fashioned way. I bought you some notebooks and graph paper. You can sort through it and figure out what you think you'll need."

"No electricity?" She wondered if they had lights and a heater, a bathroom and a shower. Didn't want to think of life without running water.

"Nope." Brody, hands in pockets, rocked back on his heels. "Sorry. I know it makes extra work for you. Carr is taking your stuff to mom's house. No reason for you to pay for a hotel room you're not using."

"Okay, makes sense." Minutes later Sadie looked out on a clear blue sky. No breeze flowed through the streets to help cool the day. But the sun now hung just above the horizon. It would be dark soon. "Do you have flashlights?"

Brody guided her to the Watering Hole. "Don't need flashlights. Will be able to see just fine. The moon will be out to light the way. Eat big. It's going to be a long time before you get breakfast," he said as they entered.

Sadie was too excited to feel hungry, but she understood what Brody said. She would eat as much as she could. "Okay, I can eat, but I don't have good night vision even with the moonlight."

"Trust me. I won't let anything happen to you."

The air in the bar seemed heavy. Sports channels could be viewed from different televisions. Crowd noise blared from each TV.

They found an out of the way corner table and ate their meal in relative silence. She wasn't sure what to say. A million issues swirled in her head. Her mind bounced from the questions she wanted to ask Brody to the ones she needed to ask his great grand father.

For a moment she leaned back in her chair and closed her eyes, wondering about the upcoming trip.

"How long will it take? To get there, I mean? Did you already tell me? Does your great grandfather know we're coming?" Geez, was she losing her mind or what? Random questions were not her style. She was always so organized, but the sight of Brody sent a myriad of emotions exploding within.

Brody took her hand in his and with his gorgeous smile, "Two full nights of travel. We will stop at a cave I know of."

"Hope there's nothing in the cave," she muttered, enjoying the feel of his hand surrounding hers.

"I'll make sure there are no other inhabitants before we enter. It will be cool inside and we'll miss the heat of the day." He let go of her hand then looked to the door as a shadow crossed the threshold.

She inhaled a deep breath as a tremor of excitement swept through her. Carr stood framed in the doorway, his broad shoulders nearly filling the opening. "Is Carr going with us?"

"He's driving the horse trailer. That's as far as he goes. When we are ready to come back, he will meet us."

"I see. Don't you think it would be safer if he rode along?" Terrified of the night and the feelings she had for Brody, a third person in this expedition would be welcome.

"Perhaps, but I don't see any danger as long as I'm with you and..." he paused for a moment, his gaze focused on her. "I want you all to myself."

"Selfish?"

"Entirely."

She laughed. "What about when we arrive at our destination? She arched one eyebrow.

"I will find a way to get some alone time. Great grandfather will allow it." They finished eating then walked to the stables at the far end of town.

Outside the air was hot and dry. Sadie watched as the brothers loaded the horses into the trailer for the ride out of town. Butterflies ripped through her insides like a category four hurricane.

"I hope I can do this," she muttered.

"I know you can," Brody stood beside her. She jumped, startled by his closeness. So engrossed in her thoughts, she had not seen him or expected him to show up behind her.

"Love your confidence in me," she slanted him a pointed stare.

"Watch your step," he said as he helped her into the truck. His hand on her arm was gentle yet firm. The feeling sent heated shivers and torrid memories of the sex they'd shared a few hours ago.

"That's an understatement." Sadie stretched to put her foot on the metal plate then grabbed the door handles to pull herself up. Brody's hand was strategically placed on her butt, and she was sure she heard him chuckle.

"I'm lovin' every second," he told her then laughed outright.

Carr settled in the rear seat, and a few seconds later Brody sat behind the wheel. The engine rumbled to life.

"How long 'till I'm learning how to ride a horse?" Sadie asked as she wove her fingers together. Nausea rolled in her gut and all her emotions seemed to be in turmoil. Excitement had been replaced with trepidation.

"An hour but it'll be easy. You're a natural."

"You know this how?" Sadie stared hard at Brody, waiting for him to enlighten her.

"Intuition."

"Men's intuition? No such thing." Sadie poked his arm. She couldn't help but enjoy the verbal exchange and it helped keep her mind off the knowledge she was about to learn how to ride a horse. He was always a challenge.

"Hey! Watch it. That hurt." He laughed a deep belly laugh then slanted one eyebrow upward.

"Yeah and I'm the queen of Sheba." Sadie sat back, her arms crossed over her chest and gazed at the scenery passing them by. Struck by the beauty of the rugged landscape, she wondered how this journey would change her life. Steep cliffs rose on both sides. A small creek dotted with rocks flowed toward the ocean. They followed the stream up river.

It didn't seem like an hour before they were unloading the truck and Brody was showing her how to saddle her horse. "What's her name?" she asked, looking over her shoulder at the man she was now entrusting with her life.

"Sheba," Brody said and laughed again.

"You're kidding, right?" It seemed everything was funny to Brody.

He shrugged broad well-muscled shoulders, "No joke."

"Okay, Sheba, it's just you and me, girl. I've faith in you. No sudden movements, okay?" Just then Sheba shifted and Sadie grabbed for the thingy in front of her.

"Take the reins," Brody's voice was the epitome of calm. "She hasn't started walking yet. But she is checking you out. Don't show any signs of fear because she'll sense it and take advantage."

Sadie inhaled a long and very deep breath, searching for the courage she needed to go through with this. She was ready to jump ship and race in the opposite direction. But she absolutely did not want

Brody to think she was a coward. More for her to gain courage than for Brody, "I can do this."

Brody and his horse assumed the lead. "I don't know what to do." Sheba fell in behind them.

"Sheba's going to do everything for you."

"Okay," her voice was unsteady but she did feel a bit more confident. After all, she was still on Sheba. But she didn't have a clue what she was going to do if Brody picked up the pace and Sheba followed suit.

Seconds turned to minutes and minutes to hours as they rode. The sky darkened and she thought she saw animals following them. But each time she looked the shadows vanished from sight. Somehow she felt warmed by their presence. No evil surrounded them; at least nothing that was tangible.

A full moon hung on the horizon and a tiny breeze ruffled her hair.

"Ready to stop for a midnight treat," Brody spoke looking over his shoulder. "Don't know about you, but I'm famished."

"What do you have in mind?" Her stomach growled at the thought of food. She imagined a big juicy hamburger.

"Momma's fingerlickin' good fried chicken. She packed a basket full of it and a canteen of cool clear water."

"I can't wait. Haven't had fried chicken for so long," she moved a bit on Sheba. For the last hour she'd tried to readjust her position so she wasn't uncomfortable. Nothing was working. "But..." she paused, wondering how she could approach the subject. "If I get off this beast, I'm not sure I can get back on it."

"We can walk a little, get the kinks out before we mount up again. I forgot you aren't used to riding."

"My butt hasn't forgotten a thing." Her concern was real. He intended to ride until the sun rose and that meant another couple of hours. A loud scream penetrated the stillness of the hour. "What..." She rose up on the horse and searched the surrounding area for the source.

"You won't see anything," Brody told her. "But it's nothing to worry about."

"How..."

"Jaguar, they won't attack us."

"They," Once again, she'd just been reduced to one-liners. "And you know this how?"

"I'm sure, come on, we'll stop in a few minutes. There's a stream up ahead and the horses will have some grass to chow down on as well as water."

"Can we rest for a little while?" Sadie rubbed the small of her back with one hand. She ached everywhere.

"An hour, you can take a nap if you want or I can give you a massage," his voice was smooth, suave, and entirely too polished.

"What are you really thinking?"

"I'm a thinkin' you need your rest. It's all good. I'm not going to attack. We need to make it to the cave before the sun gets hot."

"Maybe I'm disappointed."

He roared with laughter. "When we arrive at our little cave, I'm just going to have to change that frustration."

"I hope you do." Her spirits picked up just thinking about what they would do together.

His hands at her waist, he helped her from her horse. Taking her hand in his, he led her to a grassy spot.

"Rest or walk first?"

"Walk," she said. This wasn't the first time they had stopped. He'd been caring and considerate even though she was sure he could ride all night.

"The horses need their rest too," he massaged her neck and shoulder muscles.

"Hmm... you work magic with your fingers."

"I promise I will show you more as soon as we can."

"How much farther?" she changed the subject. Thinking about the things he could do with not only his hands but his mouth and tongue—and teeth left her heart racing.

"A couple of miles. We should easily be there before dawn." His kisses traced the path he'd just taken with his hands.

"Oh my..."

Sure she could feel his grin, she turned. His lips found hers for a brief kiss.

"Come on," he spread a blanket on the ground then unsaddled both horses. "You can use this for a pillow. He tossed her a saddlebag.

"Thanks, what are you going to do?"

"Stand guard."

"I thought you said we didn't have anything to be afraid of."

"Just precautionary. Must go back to my roots."

"I see, and your roots are..." she said and curled up to rest. She knew she couldn't sleep, but she closed her eyes and thought of her work. Then she listened to the sounds of the night. They were soft and a bit muted, but at one point she was sure she heard Brody speaking and someone else replying. She shook off the thought and wondered if she had fallen asleep and perhaps had been dreaming.

The sound of a woman's scream left her bolting to a sitting position. "What!" her hand rested on her chest and she could barely inhale a breath of air.

~ * ~

Akando, the Chullachaqui, looked over the dry parched earth, impatience and fury growing. Almost a mile away from her campsite, he couldn't even watch her. He wanted Sadie yesterday, had almost had her two years ago in Peru. He'd followed her to the States. Found her twitter account and hacked it. But she'd changed her password so many times he hadn't been able to keep up with her.

"Sadie, you're mine, not Brody McKenna's--that damn shapeshifter."

Brody's brother and sister rode shotgun. He hadn't expected Brody to relish company on this crazy mission into the unpopulated Sierra Madres. Alone, he would have been able to lure Sadie away.

Now it would be more difficult. When he approached the campsite, he'd been blocked by one of the McKenna siblings. Carr, the bigger of the two had sprung in front of him and with a low growl, warned him away.

"You will find the right time." Celinda glided next to him, her hand on his shoulder. "Although I'd rather have you all to myself, I understand your need. Perhaps, I can lure the McKenna little brother away too."

"Whatever." Akando shifted to a more comfortable position. The pair headed south and they would encounter cliffs and caves. He figured they would walk along the creek bed.

"You're taking this too seriously." Celinda stood then and walked toward the shapeshifter's camp. "We could always go back to Peru."

"Not without Sadie."

"You could walk right in, fight the guy and take her. If you got to him before he has time to shift..." Celinda grinned the smile of the devil incarnate.

"You forget his brother and sister are here." He tossed a rock and watched it skitter across the ground.

"I'll go then. I'm not afraid."

"Hah! You won't get within one hundred yards."

"Bet?" She lifted an eyebrow.

"No, I don't want you to get hurt trying." He watched her walk away from him then rose to race after her.

A screech that pierced the night filled him with terror. One of the cats sat on a tree branch above them the other in their path. The sound threatened enough for Celinda to turn and walk back.

Chapter Four

Brody touched her shoulder. "It's all right. Everything is okay. It was just one of those pesky jaguars I told you about a few hours ago." He looked to the horizon and scowled, knowing it was his siblings. "Come on, time to rise and shine then get to that cave."

And the hot springs then with any luck, the best damn sex I've ever known. And hopefully those two pesky cats, Lyn and Carr will stay away, or he'd have their hides.

Cliffs rose on both sides of the creek meandering through the canyon. After their rest, they had walked their horses down a trail to the bottom of the gorge. Now they mounted and rode. In the distance, thunder reverberated through the hot dry air.

"We'll be there in about fifteen minutes." Brody pointed up stream. He could just make out the dark hole that signified the cave. He wanted to get there soon before they encountered any lightning strikes. The sky above sported an eerie glow, one that spoke of a thunderstorm.

Sadie blew an errant piece of hair from her face. "Good, I want to make some notes. Maybe write in my journal."

"About what? You have a journal? Can I read it?" She looked nervous. Perhaps she guessed at the growing tension in the air. And he knew he pushed his luck asking to read a lady's private thoughts. But all she could do was turn him down.

"More descriptive than anything else. The plants, rocks and the terrain we have passed through. I want to jot down something about everything were seeing right now. And no, you can't read my journal."

He watched her as she seemed to take note of their surroundings. Her keen mind, even in the darkness, seemed to never stop. He shrugged off her no, hoping that soon it would change to a maybe.

"I can help if you want. I know the names of most of the plants and the rock formations the natives used to use to tell them where they were and the plants they used as medicine. Gramps knows more than anyone."

"I'd like that." She shaded her eyes with her hand and looked upward. "Do you think we're in for a storm? I smell rain in the air. That thunder sounded distant, but..."

"Yes." He didn't want to mince words with her. "We should see some explosive lightning strikes. But the storm's about two hours away."

"You're not worried?"

"We'll have shelter, so, no. But first I plan on cooking breakfast. Don't know about you but that bit of chicken a few hours ago has burned off. I'm famished." *In more ways than one, a little lovin' after we eat and I'll be a satisfied man.*

"I need to stretch my sore muscles. Don't think I've ever exercised for so long." With her hands on the back of her hips, Sadie arched her back and Brody silently groaned as he watched her sleek body and all of her curves as she displayed them just for him.

"You can do that any time." He grinned and felt the devil inside surface. The need to touch and kiss inflamed all of his senses.

"What?" Her attention shot to Brody and the look on her face was worth a picture.

Her innocence always astounded him. She had no idea what her gestures did to his already overactive mind and his hard cock.

"Move like you just did, like a beautiful kitten." He noticed the flush of her cheeks. Get a hold of yourself, buddy.

"I just stretched." The words laced with indignation made him grin.

"That's all it takes to remind me of yesterday, your bed, and your naked body next to mine. Or did you forget?"

"I remember..." Sadie walked toward him. A seductive grin spread across her face. "I remember everything about you, especially the rosettes on your body. Are they tattoos?"

God, but he wanted to be inside her head and know what she thought. "Best be ready for some more of that. I'm not going to waste the entire day on sleep. And, uh...for lack of a better word they're tattoos." Yup, he meant to make Sadie his, completely his.

Building the campfire was accomplished, and a few seconds later Brody had bacon sizzling in a frying pan and coffee perking on some hot embers. He pulled out a few bagels and handed one to Sadie.

"My stomach is growling." She broke off a piece and popped it in her mouth. "Got any cream cheese in your bag of goodies?"

"You've got to be kidding." He looked up from what he was doing and laughed.

"Can't fault me for trying." She shrugged slim shoulders. He so wanted them exposed to his gaze. He knew how they felt against his lips and how she tasted. Her scent floated on the soft breeze. God, but she always smelled so good, like a lemon grove.

To keep himself from throwing her on the bedroll and doing her before breakfast, he focused his attention to the bacon. Turning it a couple more times before he looked up, "Crisp or extra crispy?"

"Extra crispy." She rummaged through his backpack and found

mugs. A few minutes later she'd poured two cups of coffee then sat on a log, sipping the heady brew.

Brody placed the bacon strips on a tin plate before handing it to her. "Makes a good sandwich with the bagels."

She watched him assemble the food then did the same. "Good lord, this is fantastic."

"All food tastes better when you've been on the trail. How do you feel? Any bumps or bruises? I could do a thorough search." He waggled his eyebrows at her, hoping to make her laugh.

"Strangely energized."

Brody finished his meal and his coffee then waited for Sadie to do the same. When she did, he held his hand out to her. She rose, dusting her palms off on her jeans then took his hand.

An instant need to protect swamped Brody. "Come, I want to show you something." He scooped up his backpack and like a man in heaven, walked along the creek bed towards the cave. When he whistled, the horses followed.

"What is it?" She scrambled a bit to keep up with his strides so he slowed his pace.

"You, my sweet sexy one will have to wait 'til we get there." He wrapped his arm around her head and covered her eyes. The risqué tune he hummed had him grinning from ear to ear.

"That's not fair," she protested, but he listened to the laughter in her voice. He heard her inhale a breath of air, as she seemed to try for patience.

"Watch out for that rock. Pick your feet up." His warning came a bit too late. She stumbled but he did enjoy catching her. "Steady."

"Where..." She started to say, circling his waist with her arm.

We're here," he uncovered her eyes then moved so he saw the expression on her face. Holding his breath and clenching his fists at his sides, he waited in anticipation.

They reached the cave and walked inside. It was as beautiful as he remembered. The eerie darkness was relived by a steady glow from mineral formations deep inside.

"Oh my," she whispered as she stepped forward, her hands outstretched as if she wanted to touch all of the shimmering golden lights that glittered in the back of the cave. "Is that a hot springs?" Sadie walked closer, turning a three-sixty degree circle in order to take in the entire picture.

"Do you like it?" His query set his mind in a tailspin, different scenarios sweeping through his head. What if she didn't... What if she hated the cave and wanted nothing to do with the hot springs? What if she was claustrophobic?

Get a grip...

"I've never seen anything that can compare. The lights, they're gorgeous. The rising steam casts a surreal glow." She moved closer to the cave wall still reaching out her hands then turned her attention to the water, and bending down, she scooped up a handful. "So nice—this will go a long ways to ease the aches and pains my muscles have incurred from the ride. Stretching for a moment, once again Brody found himself treated to her beautiful curves.

"You can touch them, the lights, but the wall just feels like rock." He walked with her, his feet treading lightly beneath him. His insecurities, the few he had, surfaced all at the same time. His future lay here with this woman. But he wondered if she would accept him when he told her the truth. He meant to explain everything to her. The clan history and how the McKennas came to the Sierra Madres.

"Perhaps I shouldn't touch but let my imagination play with their color and their sheen. I can envision thousands of flickering lights floating around me. It's almost like fireworks when the colors are at their most brilliant." She closed her eyes then opened them again. "Do you like them?"

"I never saw these lights like you just described, and I would not have brought you here if I didn't think this was one of the most beautiful sights I have seen," he murmured as he wrapped his arm around her again then pulled her close. Sharing this moment with her meant the world to him. It was just one of several secrets he intended to disclose as time traveled forward. But for now he would savor this moment.

"Closing my eyes and letting everything swirl in my head is like nirvana to the soul." Sadie pressed her body close to his. Good God, but she was as soft as he was hard. When he closed his eyes, he pictured her naked and giving herself to him. Her skin was so soft, her body perfection.

The only way they could be closer was for his cock to find its place inside her.

Soon, you pesky little devil. I don't want her to think all I want from my relationship with her is sex. No, I want so much more. One night is not enough and one lifetime is not enough.

"When I look at you, I feel as if I have crossed to the other world. The peace and contentment settling around me was confusing at first, but now I think I'm beginning to understand what the elders have foretold." This was the first time he comprehended how his clan found their mates. How they sensed the completeness when they met their life's partner. Without Sadie, he was an empty shell.

She moved away slightly but he would have none of it. Turning her, he lifted her chin just high enough so he could look into her eyes. They sparkled with pleasure and beckoned him.

"Now you're scaring me. That's a lot of information for me to..."

But her words were cut off when his lips molded against hers. The warmth of her arms wrapped around his neck and the heat of his tongue inside her mouth sent a primal sound rumbling from inside. His loud purr echoed around the cavern and swept all thought from his mind.

As if Mother Nature inhaled the electricity passing between Brody and Sadie, shafts of light from the storm penetrated the cave, and the thunderous roar from outside seemed to engulf him.

In sync with them, the opening of the cave lit again as bolts of light seared the earth outside. Fat drops of rain pummeled the ground. More lightning hit the earth and energy sizzled around them. He felt her surprise. She pressed closer to him. For a few moments they watched. Awe for the strength and power of nature intrigued.

"It's beautiful," he said.

He turned her and pressed his hands against the small of her back then slipped his hands inside her skimpy t-shirt, sliding them upward against bare flesh. This much of Sadie was not enough Sadie.

Spreading his legs he pulled her between them then unclasped her bra. He lifted his mouth from hers for just a second. "Raise your arms," In a quick move he pulled her shirt up and over her head. Brody let his breath rush out. The sight of her pale breasts with budding pink nipples, in the muted light of the cavern sent heat rushing through him. A molten hot inferno swept within.

"Sweet, sexy Sadie you never disappoint me." He licked a finger then lightly touched one nipple then the other. His groan of pleasure reverberated throughout the cave.

"Brody, please..." she whispered.

"Please what," he asked, teasing and tantalizing her body with each word.

"Fuck me," she told him. "I want to feel you deep inside me." Her words came out in a sexy pant that sent another current of energy sizzling within.

"Fuck you? Language, little darlin' language. Of course I will."

Time was too short; he wanted to be inside her now.

Suddenly her hands were under his shirt. He didn't help. "If you don't raise your arms, I'm going to tear your damn shirt off."

He let out a roar of laughter then lifted his arms high. She wasn't tall enough to get it over his head. As she stretched and jumped to disrobe him, he reveled in the sensations her breasts caused as they lightly brushed against his chest. With a groan, "You're killin' me, honey."

"Then help..." Her words sounded indignant and her lips were pouty, tempting a ravishing kiss.

He pulled his shirt off then reached for the zipper of her jeans. Before she could say anything, she was naked in front of him. Then he slipped from his pants and swept her into his arms.

Wading into the hot springs, he settled on a low shelf just made for sitting. "Hmm..." he purred, "where to start?" Brody felt sweat break out on his brow. He knew what he must do. He had to find a way to convince her to stay with him in his mountains, a way to tell her about his clan, as well as his supernatural powers. If he couldn't convince her to stay with him, he might loose her. He couldn't risk that.

But right now he had something else on his mind. His cock was hard and pulsing. When he reached below the water to slip a finger inside her walls, she was wet with her cream.

Sadie moaned softly against his throat. She nibbled his neck with her soft little lips and moist tongue. Biting him gently, sent his body into tremors that were hard to control. Her hands kneaded his shoulders with a feverish intensity.

"You have tiny little claws," he murmured against her ear.

"Hmm..."

Raising her chin, he found her mouth and molded his to hers, opening it with his tongue and pushing forward with a primal rhythm. His fingers inside her joined the rhythm. She bucked and arched against him and he felt her shudder, her body shaking.

She responded sweetly and with so much passion, imitating the thrusts of his tongue with hot forays of her own.

"You are so fuckin' hot, Princess." He whispered against her cheek. "My perfect sexy Sadie."

"Brody, please, finish..." was all she said and her voice broke on the words. "I can't..."

"Dear God." He kissed her again, and as he did so one hand slipped around her body to cup her breast. The texture so tantalizing he was hard pressed to contain himself.

He gazed into her eyes then bowed to lick a nipple, all the while he moved his other hand to give attention to her clit. Her tiny scream brought a grin and he returned to her mouth for an instant, silencing her but not her body as she writhed and twisted in pattern with his seduction.

But he couldn't resist her breasts, and soon he touched the tip of his tongue to the nipple again, flicked it back and forth until she grabbed his hair and forced his mouth hard against her. He sucked her nipple deep inside his mouth, biting gently. Fuck, but he had meant to take this slow, give her so much pleasure she would beg him to take her inside. He wanted her to climax over and over again before he entered her.

His fingers delved into her cream. He parted her then teased her clit until she could hold back no longer. Watching her swaying breasts, her sexy tongue darting over kiss-swollen lips, Brody continued to stroke her swollen nub. Suddenly she moaned, her body shuddered and bucked then tremors rocked her body. She held tight to him, pressing against his flesh until her body calmed and she let her head rest against his chest.

"Brody, you've got to stop doing this to me." Her breath was slowing and the words she spoke were weak.

"You don't like me to touch you here and here?" he said with a laugh as his fingers once again danced over her body and she moved in perfect synchronization.

"I'm as fragile as a kitten." Her body arched again and he laughed low and deep.

"Nice analogy," he knew the time would be right. Soon, he would tell then show her who he was and what he could do.

"What about you?" Her fingers closed over him. "You're still hard as a rock. I want to help."

"So, it's my turn now," he said, slipping two fingers inside her and finding more cream. "Are you ready for me? All of me? Tell me now if you don't want me inside you." He gave her time to answer. She nodded. He left her long enough to retrieve protection from the pocket of his jeans. Opening the condom wrapper, he put it on and in a moment's time was deep inside her.

He was lost in the mystery and the magic that surrounded Sadie, his woman. The scent of lemons blended with the electricity of the early morning, floating upward from the hot springs.

"Brody..." His name floated on the hot silver mist surrounding them.

His mouth slanted hungrily across hers. He nibbled on her lower lip, his teeth biting down gently and tugging. He stroked inside her mouth while he tried to hold himself still. His arms circled her back and pulled her tighter until they seemed to meld as one.

Brody pulled away from her, watching her, studying her, knowing he had to rely on patience. But her kiss-swollen lips were like an aphrodisiac calling to him.

Her fingers raked down his chest. Feminine nails slid across male nipples in an age-old dance. He held himself rigid in a futile attempt to keep the pace slow. He shook with the need for her and to feel their release.

He kissed her eyes, her cheeks, the corners of her mouth, then deepened the kiss. Nibbling on the tender flesh, playing chase with her tongue, he kissed her hard and she responded. He knew she wanted more and he would give her the world. He kissed her again and again.

"My sweet, sexy Sadie."

"Brody..."

He could wait no longer. His body flexed and she followed the rhythm he set. He drove deep inside her, stroking longer, deeper, harder, until she cried out.

Pleasure exploded within him, liquid fire raged through him. "Sadie." He whispered his name even while he shook with the fever pitch she sent spiraling inside his body.

Slowly their bodies calmed. She raked her fingernails over the taut muscles of his back as if exploring. Long, quiet minutes passed, and his cock slipped from inside her. He settled her on his lap, holding tight to her, not wanting to ever let her go. She turned to face him a lazy smile on her lips and he studied her and wondered what she thought. With gentleness he lifted her hair and buried his face within.

"Lemon. Even your hair carries the scent of lemons.

Brody touched her collarbone then down farther. His touch to her nipple brought it to a rapid and sudden peak. He laughed softly and knew the sound of a man well satisfied. His cock hardened and they made love once more.

~ * ~

Sadie sat cross-legged on the sleeping pallet and watched Brody stride from the cave. He moved with an effortless grace, his muscles working as one. The storm had vanished, moved to the east.

She found herself fascinated with him, his family and the legends. Something else about him intrigued her though. He wasn't honest about everything, about his family. He had a secret he wanted to tell her.

With a grimace and a sigh she retrieved her journal and pen from her backpack and settled in to jot down a few things before she slept. She wouldn't pry but she hoped he would confide soon.

Dear journal,

I wonder at the hold Brody has over my mind and body. I watch him and feel things I just don't understand. Every time I look at him, and I mean every time, I want to have sex with him. I need him inside me, deep inside, and I want to climax in his arms. He completes me. Dear God, just writing this down has given me those same desires. I am wet and ache for his touch.

What is it about him that makes me forget my life's goals? Sometimes I think that if he asked me right now to stay here with him, I would say yes. My aspirations are more important to me than a good fuck. And that's just what he gives me—sex I can't stop thinking about and wanting more.

Is there more to Brody? What lies beneath the surface of that man? He is quiet and he's quick to laugh. But...

I truly believe there is something he is not telling me. Secrets are not appropriate. But I have only known him for a couple of days. I haven't confided in him. I really haven't told him anything about myself. Indeed I know more about him than he does about me.

Why didn't he tell me where he was off to? A run no doubt. But I have the distinct feeling he is meeting someone and that perhaps Carr followed us after all. Several times when we stopped I was sure I heard voices. But I was too tired to pursue the topic. Unless Brody returns soon, I will be asleep then we will be eating and having fantasmic sex, then sleeping again, eating, sex then riding.

My goodness where is the energy coming from? It feels as if Brody has a never ending flow and such a huge appetite for life. He loves everyone and I love no one. Every one I have ever tried to love has hurt me or failed me when I needed them. When my mother left us, I was devastated. I learned a long time ago that I can only rely on myself.

Brody has told me the remainder of the journey is easier and shorter. We will be at his great grandfathers way before dawn if we leave at dusk. His great grandfather must be an incredible man. Must have seen so much life. I am eager to meet him.

Alas, but I'm rambling. I must search out information for my grant. If I receive money, I will return here and perhaps get to know Brody better. Knowing him would be counter-productive. Nothing can come of this strange relationship we have.

Except good sex.

"You still awake?" Brody's sexy, sleek body strode through the opening of the little cave and straight toward her. "That could be dangerous. Might be hours before I let you close your eyes." He sent her a delicious wink.

"Where did you go?" Sadie shut her journal and placed it in her backpack. She felt a bit awkward. And she definitely didn't want to talk about the thoughts she'd written down. Knowing more about the man who enticed and intrigued her, high on her agenda.

"Needed to feel the sun on my back." He rummaged through his pack until he found an orange. "And, I wanted to stretch my legs, work out a few kinks in my shoulders and neck before we slept. The air is clean and fresh right now. The rain cleared the dust and smoke from the skies."

58

She watched him peel it then hand a slice to her. The juice was sweet and delicious. He bent over and licked a drop from her lips. Then, in pure Brody fashion, he nibbled his way down her neck.

"That's not a good idea." Sadie scooted backwards, distancing herself from him. Until she understood him a bit more, she hoped she could keep him at arms length. If she were to be realistic, she knew that was impossible. They seemed to have an unbreakable and unexplainable bond between them.

"Last night I could have sworn I heard voices," she challenged him for the truth. When the moon was low on the horizon, that third time we stopped. "I heard you talking to someone. Who was it?"

He grimaced then smiled at her. "You did. Carr didn't keep his promise. Thought I needed someone ridin' shotgun. Sis came along too, as Carr's sidekick. As if one of my siblings following us wasn't enough."

"I did hear a woman too. Where did they stay last night during the storm?" She bit into the slice of orange, staring at all that male flesh in front of her. Muscles she wanted to trace and explore more thoroughly.

"Yeah, he dragged little sis along with him. She's the one who is always up for an adventure. Her twin would rather stay at home. There are a lot of caves around here. None so beautiful as this one though."

"So—why didn't they ride with us?" she asked. "I'd like to meet sis, does she have a name?" This was the diversion she needed.

"I told Carr earlier and I still mean it, I want you to myself. If you haven't noticed yet, I'm not a sharin' kind of guy. We call her Lyn but her name is Lyonesses. It's Celtic for little lion." He sat down next to her and wrapped his arm around her. The kiss to her forehead was not sexual but somehow comforting.

"Who are you really—Brody McKenna?" Her boldness startled

her. Did she want to know that much about him? It might make leaving harder than she assumed it would be. Despite her work, maybe because of it, she wanted to be with him. She knew he could introduce her to the people she would need to interview if she were to get the grant. The great grandfather was just the first of many natives in the area who could give her information.

"Curious about me? I like that." He pulled her so he held her close. Her back was against his chest and she sat between his legs. His hands stroked her arms then settled at her waist for a moment. But they didn't remain there for long. It seemed Brody still wanted to explore every part of her.

"Very." He handed her another slice of orange. Sadie let her head fall back and closed her eyes, reveling in the peace of the moment, the quiet solitude in the cave. They were volatile together. It seemed they burned hot and fast, igniting in a second and always simmering. Yet the serenity she felt when he was near was something she'd never experienced.

"I like that in my woman. Curiosity is a sign of intelligence."

Then it sounded as if he purred.

"I'm not your woman." Sadie realized she had already given way too much of herself to this man. But she didn't want to pull back and she didn't want to be any man's woman. She was her own person and had worked way too long to become Brody's plaything. Confusion settled in her head. She asked herself what she really wanted and found no answer.

She untangled herself from his arms then strode to the opening of the cave. Looking out at the rocky terrain, she thought about the man behind her and how this landscape must have molded him, hardened him then perfected him.

"Are you afraid, Sadie?" She prayed he wouldn't follow her, touch her. She would melt just like she always did.

"I need to think," she told him.

"Don't think, just feel." He was beside her, his footsteps so quiet she hadn't heard him.

She didn't turn but she stepped away. "That's the problem, Brody. That's all I've been doing—feeling. I've let you...well, it's all just happening too fast. I can't breathe and my heart doesn't stop racing."

"Hasn't anyone ever told you that breathing is over rated," he purred next to her ear then traced the shell with his tongue.

"Brody," she stepped into the sun and immediately regretted it. Shielding her eyes from the blinding glare, this time she turned to meet his penetrating gaze. "We can't just fuck each other until we can't move. There has got to be more to a relationship or there isn't one."

His eyes grew dark and brooding before he turned from her. "You don't believe we have more? You think all we have together is sex?" He looked over his shoulder at her. "If that' what you think, I don't know how to convince you otherwise, Princess. But I'm gonna die trying."

"You're angry. I just think we should take things a bit slower. You're a nice and caring person, Brody McKenna, and I appreciate all you've done and are doing for me." Her heart felt as if it had been ripped into two pieces.

He was so still she couldn't believe how he changed, the expression on his face, his lips, his eyes. "No, I'm not angry," he said on a whisper. "Just searching my thoughts and wondering what it will take."

"I don't understand."

"I know," he said. "I will think of the words."

~ * ~

"I saw the devil, actually there were two of them." Carr strode with purposeful strides away from the cave where Brody and Sadie had settled for the day.

Did you tell big Bro?" Lyn bit down on a piece of chicken as she walked toward the tiny opening on the cliff in front of her.

"No, but I will. He told me to stay away from the cave. I value my life so that's the plan." He looked at the sky. "Storm's on the way. We're going to have to find shelter."

"There's another cave a couple of miles away. If we hurry, we can get there before we get wet." She pointed toward a pinhole of darkness in front of them.

"I'm worried about Brody and Sadie. Someone needs to stand guard." Carr had second thoughts about abandoning his brother. With the Amazonian devil and his sidekick close by, he didn't want to leave them alone.

"No, that's not the way they work. They lure their victims. And I don't think any Amazonian devil could entice Sadie out of Brody's arms. If this storm proves to be as volatile as it looks, no one will be outside during it."

"How do you know so much? This is the first time I've heard any real information or facts about such a creature."

"Demons 101 on the internet. I Googled them and ran across this one. Characteristics match. Then I called great grandfather. He confirmed my suspicions. Seems this isn't the only one that has been seen in these parts. There's a woman too and we saw her. Trust me, it's safe for them to spend the night together unguarded. I wonder if the two devils are after them or just the man."

"Can only speculate on that. I feel the first raindrop. Let's get a move on." Carr put his hand to his eyes to shield the sun. With the speed of light clouds gathered on the horizon and darkened.

The sky thundered and lit with explosive force. Strikes of lightning pummeled to the earth. Electricity seemed to singe the air.

"Good God," Carr said, "this could be the mother of all storms. I'll race you to the cave."

With haste, they gathered the food, and after packing it away, set off for the second cave.

Lyn brushed the raindrops from her shirt and laughed. "I think we just out ran the devil."

"Yeah, we got here just in time." Carr settled the horses in a corner of the cave then gave them their feed.

"Nothing more to do than wait it out." Lyn watched the eerie glow.

Carr sat down beside her and wrapped his arm around her. "You're trembling. You know there is nothing to be afraid of."

Outside, silhouetted by the light, a shadow of a man stood.

Chapter Five

"Gramps is resting." Lyn rose from the couch in the living room. Lyn and Carr had arrived first. "He said to make yourselves at home."

"Sadie, this is Lyonesse. We call her Lyn for short." Brody was abrupt with the introductions.

Sadie held out her hand in greeting, and Lyn grasped Sadie's hand in hers. "I'm glad to meet you. Brody hasn't told me anything about you. I have to pry things from him." She winked at Sadie and grinned at her brother.

"Me too, I'm eager to get to know you. He hasn't told me anything about you either. Brody is a man of few words but this is ridiculous." Lyn walked to the hallway then turned around as if to study Sadie and Brody, a strange expression on her face. Before a second passed, she returned and sat down.

Sadie turned in a complete circle. "This is very nice."

"Gramps has good taste. He likes Native American art and Brody loves the flute. Gramps taught him how to play. Now what would you like to do?" Lyn asked as she stepped back into the living area.

"Food then a bath. I'm starving. Thanks."

"Sleep?" Lyn nodded toward the bedrooms. "I'd think you'd be exhausted."

"A nap later but I'd like to look around. I'm too intrigued by all of this and your great grandfather. I really want to talk with him."

Brody paced the room, glancing from Lyn to Sadie. He still didn't have a plan, and his nerves sent tremors through his body. After the conversation in the cave, his confidence was shot. Telling her about his ability to shift into cat form could be a deal breaker. But somehow he sensed the shield Sadie had put up around herself. She was guarding her heart from him, and he had to find a way to break through. He'd like to know why that barrier was so thick too. But that would come in time. First, she had to learn to trust him then he wanted her to understand a relationship with him meant more than great sex.

"Let's go see what's in the fridge." Brody's hunger always got the best of him. He needed food then Sadie. Usually it was the other way around. Right now he needed to rejuvenate his body. And he didn't have time or fortitude for Lyn and her games.

"He has electricity way out here?" Sadie looked surprised when she asked. "I guess I didn't expect the twenty-first century."

"A generator keeps things modern. Did you think you'd be scrubbing pans in the riverbed?" Brody sauntered through the living room, leading the way to the kitchen.

Sadie shrugged her slim shoulders and showed him a sheepish grin. "Guess I didn't think."

"Pancakes ok with you?" he asked as he set about assembling the ingredients and mixing up the batter.

"Yumm..." Sadie laughed and the sound filled the hole inside Brody that had formed since their last conversation.

"Good for me too," Lyn said, settling in at the table then slanting Brody an I'm staying here just too irritate you smile.

"Good, I make a mean pancake. But when we're done here, little sis, I need to speak with Sadie privately." Brody turned on the stovetop then finished cooking. He hummed when he worked and thought about Sadie and learning all he could about her.

"Really, haven't you already had a lot of private time together?" Lyn asked then winked at Sadie. "Ok, but I plan to get to know Sadie. And you're not going to stand in my way, big bro."

"Just don't tell any tall tales, alright," Brody said.

"After that, they ate with little conversation." Lost in thought, Brody wasn't sure what to do. A plan would be nice, but he had no ideas. Everything about this now felt stilted and formal. The easy camaraderie they'd known only a few hours ago had vanished. But he wasn't about to give up.

"See you later, Sadie." Lyn left the two alone.

"You said there was a shower?" Sadie put her fork down and waited for his response.

"Outdoors," he said, an idea began to take shape and a fantasy of his might be fulfilled.

"There is? Now where do I put my clothes?" She sipped the water in front of her. "Is it open or enclosed? Hot or cold? I have no idea what to think."

"Mostly we just take a bathrobe and a towel. It's enclosed so you'll have all the privacy you need, unless you let me join you. Then..."

"I didn't bring a robe." She drummed one finger on the table then looked out the window. "Guess I'll just take a towel and soap. I assume you can send me in the right direction."

"I'll get you a towel and the robe I use when I'm here. Well, maybe a different one, mine might be too big." He rose and extended a hand to help her up. She accepted it. Hand in hand they walked to his room. His plan took on a whole new dimension.

The closet where they ended up overflowed with jeans, shirts and shoes. Rummaging through it and pulling out different items then tossing them on the floor, he finally found what he looked for.

"Here you go." He held up the robe for inspection. "My mother uses this one when she visits gramps. So it should fit ok."

"Thanks, where do I change?"

"Right here." He backed from the room, wondering if she would ask him to stay.

"Are we both sleeping here?"

"Not if you don't want to. It's entirely in your hands." Wishing and praying she would decide in his favor, his fingers itched to help her from her clothing.

She motioned for him to leave. "Go on. I can do this by myself. I know what you're thinking, and it's not going to happen right now."

"It's not like I haven't seen all of you. And you don't know my thoughts, although you're damn close." He wanted to help her undress; touch and kiss every inch.

"I told you earlier that I needed time to think. Right now I want some privacy. You have a way of making me think about nothing but you." She pointed a finger at him.

"That's the plan, my sexy princess." He grinned at her then brought her chin up to meet his lips. "A kiss before I leave you to your privacy."

He wanted this kiss to send a message to her very soul. Putting his heart and his tongue behind it, he meant to persuade and entice and let her know she needed him on a primal level. Yet he knew that on an intellectual plane he didn't have the same educational background. He didn't feel less of a person. He knew he was smart and creative; he just didn't have the college degree or that little ole masters diploma.

She met him with hot sweet passion. Her tongue delving into his mouth and her sexy little purr of pleasure bolstered his confidence. He broke away first then gave her a soft little pat on her butt.

"Get going or you won't make it to the shower. Oh, and save some water for me. I've already got other plans in my head, and they involve you and me, together, here on that bed." He wasn't going to give her a lot of time. He would be there before she could blink.

"Haven't you forgotten something?" she asked, her hands on her hips and one toe tapping with impatience.

"Okay, I'm leaving."

Brody strode outside hoping to cool off and reflect. He didn't want to make what could be the biggest mistake of his life. But he sensed she'd be okay with this. And he wanted to test her. Breaking into an easy lope, he put a mile between the house and Sadie. She would be in the shower now.

Stopping, he disrobed and folded his clothes. Impatience had him sweating. Adrenalin started to flow as he slowly began to shift to his jaguar shape. Exhilaration was the key word when he transformed. For a few seconds he stood still then sniffed the air. The breeze was clean and cool, the sun not yet dousing the earth with heat.

His tail twitched with anticipation then he ran, the speed like an aphrodisiac to his soul. Close to the shower, he slowed. Sadie's slightly off key singing made him smile. When his eyes were closed, he could see her naked, and he knew as soon as she saw him in his human form she would be aroused and her cream would flow.

Her back turned away, she didn't see him until he was inches from her. As if sensing a presence, she spun then froze.

"My God." She backed toward the wall behind her. "Good kitty—cat. Go away."

Brody sat on his haunches, cocking his head to one side. In his feline form a grin was hard but he tried. Slanting one eyebrow upward was easier. He didn't mean to frighten her. He wanted to read her mind, get inside her thoughts.

Patience...

"D-don't eat me," she said, her hands outstretched as if that would keep him from devouring her.

Her gorgeous breasts swayed and he wanted to lick her. Damn his cat form. Maybe this wasn't such a great idea after all. His tail twitched and his purr filled the air. But he waited, needing her to know he would never hurt her. He was her friend.

"Nice kitty." Sadie's back was solidly against the wall now, her knees shaking.

She had nowhere to go. Minutes seemed to pass like hours. He knew he needed to get out of here. Another plan shaped in his head. Everything would come together. If he were to tell her about himself tonight, this was good. She would have seen that he wouldn't hurt her. He didn't want to scare her any longer. Time to finish this scenario and leave.

Brody stood and walked toward her then rubbed against her legs, purring and knowing he would be back. Oh, yes, he'd be back for more of Sadie Monroe.

"B-Brody," she tried to say. "Help...Lyn where are you?"

She was terrified and he didn't like himself very much at this moment. Then he felt her fingers on top of his head. Stroking his neck, she seemed to grow bolder. Then she scratched behind his ear. He looked at her and she seemed to be inching her way to her robe.

"I don't think I like standing naked in front of you," she said, scooting toward the opening of the shower stall and her protection. "You seem...you seem human in a strange way."

He shook his head then turned. In a quick motion, he had the towel and her robe in his teeth and dashed across the yard.

From behind him he heard her swear. He laughed inside and wondered what she would do now. Would she stay in the shower? Would she come after him all gloriously naked?

"Fuck you! Bring back my robe. It's not mine, you know."

Oh he knew. It was his now and he was going to bring it back to her—but on his terms.

~ * ~

Sadie stood in the shower, letting the water rush over her. She closed her eyes and tried to understand what had just happened. Had she truly just been in this tiny outdoor shower with a huge black jaguar? And had she rubbed his ears. And...why on earth could she think he reminded her of Brody? She had only been afraid for a few seconds.

Too...many questions and not enough answers.

She had to figure out a way to sneak back to the house without anyone seeing her, especially Carr. Butt naked was not how she wanted to proceed, but she certainly didn't have a choice.

Peeking around the door to the shower, she prayed she'd find Brody sauntering down the path. He could save her anytime. No one was there. He probably saw the whole thing and would rescue her but when he felt like it.

"Brody McKenna, if you are anywhere close, you need to get your butt to the shower, yesterday." She didn't think he was nearby, but one could always pray.

On a huff and a sigh she stood under the water again. Damn, damn and double damn. Everything happens for a reason, but she couldn't figure this one out. What possible good could come of the black cat stealing her towel and robe? Except her humiliation when she scampered from one bush to another making her way to the ranch.

"Lose something?"

His voice had never sounded so good. Relief swept through her. She turned to him. The devilish smile on his face baffled her. "It's about time you showed up. You'll never believe..."

"Hush..."

His grin melted her insides. God, why was he so handsome? She couldn't think when he was around. Her body clenched tightly in expectation of his cock deep inside. Thoughts of the hot springs filled her head.

"I found these scattered on the path." His hands rested on his unbuttoned, unzipped jeans. Then he held up the towel and robe. "Why did you drop them on the trail?"

"You wouldn't believe me." *I can't tell him a black jaguar was in the shower with me and that I rubbed its ears and there would be no way to explain how I let the cat take my robe and towel.*

"How..." He stepped closer, touching her shoulder then sliding one finger along her collarbone. Shivers of pleasure danced through her.

"Just let it go." Water washed over her face. She felt the flush of embarrassment slide down her body.

"What if I don't want to let anything go, including you?" He waved a condom wrapper in one hand and stepped toward her. In quick fluid movements he disrobed, the condom was in place and one finger was inside her. His sexual expertise amazed her. Her body began to move with the rhythm he set.

"Cream...for me, princess. Wrap your legs around me. Cradle me deep inside you and I'll do my damndest to make you moan with delight." His whisper next to her ear sent heat pumping.

She obeyed as he put a towel behind her back, pressing her against the shower wall while water poured over them. He kissed and teased her body then sent her over the edge. Seconds later her body shook with the force of her climax. Resting her head against his shoulder, she drew in long deep shuddering breaths.

"How do you do that to me?" She traced one of his tattoos, intrigued by them. "Every time we make love I come so fast. You exhaust me only to do it to me again."

"Want to practice?" he asked, sliding his hands over her back. "I got more where that came from. Remember the old saying, practice makes perfect."

"Not right now." Her voice echoed against his collarbone. No matter how tempted she was, she needed rest and she needed to meet his grandfather.

"Are you sure? We can make it a quickie." He squeezed her butt. The reflex was automatic. She moved on his cock, which was still hard and deep inside her. His lips molded across her mouth, his tongue delving inside as he slowly moved.

"Positive. And they're all quickies. Not that I'm complaining." But she groaned and wiggled against him, her breasts brushing his chest.

"Do that again and I won't have a choice but to take matters into my own hands." He pushed a little ways away from her and pulled one nipple into his mouth sucking hard and making her shudder and buck once more. "It's all good, princess. It's so damn fine. You're so perfect."

"Brody, we have to..." Her fingers wove into his hair, pulling him closer then she ran her nails across his back.

"Later, he's asleep right now anyway. Lyn says he usually gets up around noon. Gramps will answer all of your questions. For this moment you're mine." His mouth found hers.

"Brody, I won't make it until noon if we don't get out of here and get dressed." But she moved on him again, and one finger found her clit. He teased her, made her moan with pleasure. She arched into his body, thrusting her breast up and toward his mouth. He claimed one nipple and laved it with his tongue then bit gently.

"Not so fast, little princess. I just can't get rid of the feel of your naked flesh against me."

He pushed inside and she rode him again, hard and fast. She arched and shook with the pleasure. Her body trembled for what seemed like hours as sensations rocked through her.

"I can't move. I feel like a have no bones." Her breath came in shallow pants, and her body trembled and pulsed against his. Ever so slowly he pulled from her then set her on the ground.

Brody grabbed the soap. After putting a generous amount in his hands, he lathered her body. She leaned into him, letting him support her weight as once again he teased and tantalized every part of her.

"I love touching you," he purred close to her ear then licked and nibbled her there.

"Amen," she sighed. "But we have to do more than fuck each other all day long. There is more to life."

"Hmm... Once more, princess and I'll let you off the hook."

"I'll be a pool of mush on the shower floor."

"I'll carry you back to the bedroom and let you sleep."

"Promise?"

"No." They made love again, the water turning cold before he finally dried her off, dressed her in his robe and carried her back to the bedroom.

He kicked the door open and stepped inside.

"Gramps is up," Lyn said from behind him. "We've another breakfast waiting."

Sadie couldn't help but let out a tiny moan. Sleeping had been on her mind until that instant. They had been up for a long time. Well, sleep was overrated. At this moment, she felt energy flow.

"We'll get dressed and meet him in the kitchen," Brody said then turned and looked at Sadie with that wicked grin of his. Then laughed, "You are hungry, aren't you?"

"Not for what you're thinking. You nasty boy, you." Punching him on the shoulder, she wanted nothing more than to hide from Lyn. Sadie knew where Brody's sister's thoughts would travel.

A few minutes later Sadie and Brody walked through the house to the outdoor patio. Breakfast had been served on the small table that sat in the center of the space. Steaming mugs of coffee, strawberries, eggs and homemade bread along with hash brown potatoes and bacon awaited their attention.

"Eat," Gramps said then gestured with his hand toward the wonderful smelling food.

Sadie's stomach growled in anticipation, surprising her. Along with Lyn, Carr, and Brody, she filled a plate then sat down to eat.

"Delicious," she said. "Thank you so much. There is nothing like a second breakfast to get one's day off to a grand start."

"You may call me Nigan. I am the one who looks ahead." He spoke slowly, reverently. "If you listen to the wind, it will tell you your future. The wind, sky and earth will never lie to you if your heart is pure. Follow your heart and you will find eternal happiness."

"I'm not sure I understand," she said then strained to see if she could hear anything.

"In time you will." Then he turned to Brody. "Have you seen the devil slayer?"

"Now it is my turn to not understand," Brody said.

"He rides alone on a black horse and he is dressed all in black. If you saw him, you would know. There is no mistaking him for anyone else." Nigan set his fork on the table and once again looked to the sky as if seeking answers. "He is like us but different. Know that he is a good man."

"Devil slayer..." Brody pushed his hair from his eyes. "Can't say that I've heard talk of anyone with that description."

"He chases the demons of the night and sometimes the day. He has seen the Chullachaqui and seeks him out. When he finds the Amazonian devil, he will slay him." Nigan folded his hands in front of them. For a moment he looked down as if praying then faced Brody once more.

"I might have seen him our first night out. Sadie was resting and I walked a little ways from the campfire. I thought I heard something. All I saw was a dark silhouette. A coldness slithered inside of me."

"I could have seen this Amazonian devil the night of the storm." Lyn gestured with her fork. "A great bolt of lightening lit up the cave opening. Carr and I saw a ghostly silhouette of a man. At the sight of this creature, cold sliced through me like a knife."

"The devil slayer. The legends abound. He is almost—what do you call them these days—a super hero. You did not see the devil slayer, because if you did, you would not have been chilled." Nigan said pushing back his long white hair. He looked up, into the sun. "The heat feels good on my old bones. Why are you here, child? Why did you travel to the Sierra Madres?"

Sadie cleared her throat to speak. "I'm an anthropologist. My team and I are working on material to apply for a grant. We do not agree. So we each went our separate way to research individually."

"What good will that do? Separation will not give you the answers you seek. People must work together."

"We will meet in the fall and discuss the possible projects."

Sadie set her fork down. Brody reached out and placed his hand on top of hers. The gesture warmed her. She had felt the cold with the talk of the devil slayer and the Chullachaqui.

"Then you did not have a calling to these parts." Nigan stood. A deep frown grew across his brow. "You are my great grandson's mate. He is the alpha male. You must stay here."

"No," Sadie shook her head, clasping her fists tightly and withdrawing her hand from Brody's. "I don't have to do anything. Mate?" She looked at Brody whose head was downcast so she couldn't read his expression. Her heart raced and nervous energy coursed through her as anger flared.

"You must come to terms with your fate. Sooner or later you will have to." Nigan continued standing, his hands folded in front of him.

"My fate and my will are my own. I know who I am and what I want." She felt the increasing rise of her temper. She did not mean to disrespect Brody's great grandfather. But...

Brody placed his hand back on hers. "Please relax, I will explain everything. Patience, Sadie, and you will learn all that he is speaking of then you will make up your mind. No one will tell you what to do."

"My direction and purpose will not change." She stood adamant on that fact. Her research had consumed her life for the past four years. She would not let the dream vanish. And was that what Brody and Nigan asked of her? She wasn't sure.

"There is a lot you do not know. But I will teach it all to you." Brody cleared his throat then looked into the distance, shielding his eyes from the sunlight. "We can begin tonight."

"Perhaps your budding information is not something I wish to learn." Her body shook with emotion and the fear she might not have a choice. She did not want to care deeply for Brody McKenna, but she feared it might be too late. Strengthening her resolve was important.

76

"We will go to the cliffs where one can see infinity." Brody spoke softly, reverently as if this place held some religious value.

"Where is this place? It is not possible to see forever." Brody had spiked her curiosity.

"The cliffs are east of here. Not too far and the moon will guide us. It is a place of worship for those who have lived in these parts." The respect in his voice reverberated around the room.

"I concede," Sadie told him, feeling the weight of the world on her shoulders.

Immersed in a quagmire and unable to free herself, she knew determination must be the bottom line for her. Brody held such sway over her.

~ * ~

Angel McKenna, sometimes known as the devil or demon slayer, watched the flames from his smokeless cook fire spiral upwards. Eyes focused on the horizon, he wondered at his duty. Most of the time the recipients of his good deeds didn't know he'd saved their life. But Brody McKenna would need to work with him to ensure Sadie Monroe's safety. Brody would need help. The Chullachaqui was a powerful demon.

Hairs on the back of Angel's neck stood on end. With a quick move, he swiveled and drew his gun. Nothing. A shadowed movement behind a rocky cliff caught his attention. He stood, shielding his eyes to better see, his heart pounding as adrenalin raced through his veins.

A coyote...

Could be the Chullachaqui, but...

He didn't feel the cold--just a presence. He watched for minutes then set to cooking his breakfast. He poured a cup of coffee. God, but he felt old and tired of trail food. What he wouldn't give to eat a home cooked meal.

His branch of the McKenna Clan lived in New Mexico. He and his brothers were shapeshifters too, but they shifted into wolves-- strange how the world works. All the other McKennas shifted to jaguars. They were all related but... they were so very different too. Cousins, how many times removed?

He dusted his hands off on his chaps then tossed the remains of his coffee into the fire, listening to the embers hiss and spit. Not much better. Dirt seemed to cling to him.

Following the foursome from their drop off point had been interesting. He'd almost walked in on Brody and Sadie when they were in the hot tub. Lyn was a beautiful woman, but he didn't think a union between the two of them would work too well. He didn't feel a calling to her.

Prostitutes and one-night stands had seen to his physical release, but he wanted more.

So much more.

He was tired of chasing other people's demons. He wanted to chase his dreams. Perhaps this would be the end of his roaming. He prayed.

A loud cry split the air. He dropped the fork he'd been using to turn the bacon, the utensil ricocheting off the rock around his campfire.

Chullachaqui, Akando, your friend, Celinda, is not happy with you. Perhaps she knows you mean to leave her when you capture Sadie. What she doesn't know is that I won't let you hurt Sadie Monroe. She is promised to another.

Chapter Six

Brody stood at the top of Infinity Cliff, Sadie at his side. He'd wrapped his arm around her as if the gesture would keep her with him for eternity. She didn't lean into him as she usually did. The physical separation didn't alarm him as much as the emotional distance. Day by day they should be growing closer, melding as one.

Instead there was a chasm between them as deep and as wide as the Grand Canyon. A shield so thick even superman's x-ray vision wouldn't be able to penetrate its depth. He sought answers but none were forthcoming. For each step forward he took two backwards.

The sky stretched on forever. Stars blinked in the evening light and a soft wind blew across his face. He closed his eyes, letting the atmosphere settle inside and allowing his soul to cleanse.

Sadie stood stiff and tall against him. When he looked at her, her face was pale and she trembled. He didn't want to do that to her. He needed to make her happy.

"I don't get why we're here." She sounded petulant and irritable. He had hoped she would see the significance and the astounding beauty of Infinity Cliff.

"You need to see where I came from and the journey through time we travel together." He should have bit his tongue before he finished that sentence. With his words, she shifted farther away. A frigid cold swept through him. It was not the chill of the Chullachaqui but a coldness he had created.

"Brody," she turned toward him, "we've had this conversation. It isn't going anywhere. I'm not staying. I might return if this is where my team decides to study, but we might never see each other again."

For a while at least, he could ignore the negativity and think only positive thoughts. Compromise meant a great deal to him. He was more than willing to do his part. And what she didn't know was that he wouldn't rest until he called Sadie Monroe his wife.

He pointed toward the vast emptiness in front of them. His words were spoken softly and with a reverence that came deep within his heart. "The McKennas lived in the highlands of Scotland. How they came there no one knew. Some say they arrived after a long journey across Pangaea."

He inhaled a long deep breath for courage. What he was about to show Sadie could set back their relationship, could put them in jeopardy of ever moving forward.

"More folk legends?" She stepped toward the edge of the cliff then peered over it. "My God, there is no bottom."

"That is why we call this place Infinity Cliff." He wanted to laugh but held his breath instead.

"I see." She leaned farther.

His heart stopped. "Don't go so close. There are loose rocks and footing can be precarious." Sensing her interest in his family's history, he chose to go slowly, perhaps stretch out the time with her. All night with her would not be long enough. He pulled her back and closer to him. Chipping away each tiny part of her shield one tiny particle at a time would be an endeavor of hard work and love. He didn't intend to make the shield stronger, so choosing his words carefully was paramount.

"How did you come to be here and why would you leave Scotland if it was your family home?" She moved back but he saw her reluctance as well as the fact that her curiosity was not appeased.

"The McKenna Clan grew and prospered. But there was not enough room for a family who loved their freedom and needed space to roam without hindrance. Some of the other clans were not always friendly. They did not understand our need and were afraid of us."

"Who—why—would anyone stop you from wandering if you owned the land? Afraid? I don't get it."

"Those are good questions. I'm not sure I know the entire answer to any of them." Her query terrified him. Time grew closer where he would bare his soul to her and show her his other form.

Sitting down, she played with some loose sand and rocks, letting it sift through her fingers. "I feel like this dirt, falling through time with no roots and no place to call home. But for now, I like the feeling. I've never wanted responsibility to anyone but myself."

Brody wanted to shout out, this is your home. But he didn't dare. His home was wherever Sadie was. "I guess like many men some grew restless and others just wanted to chase the sunrise. Men want what is best for their families. So they pursued a dream."

Just as I pursue my dreams.

"I feel that way sometimes. I don't think men are the only ones who need to seek out other places and discover new lands or live for their dreams." She dusted her hands off on her jeans.

"Come, let's sit." He nodded toward a large rock behind them. "I suppose not. The story goes back to one of the clansmen named Alastair. He sought a wife but found no one he truly felt as one with. With each passing year he grew more desperate. In his sleep, he dreamed of the land across the ocean, America. Finally, he made the decision to travel to the US in hopes of finding a woman, the right woman, his soul mate. He wanted a wife and children, but he knew or somehow sensed no one waited for him in Scotland."

"Very romantic." She stood and tossed a rock over the cliff then paused a moment as if she waited to hear it land.

When she turned to look over her shoulder at him, he spoke. "You will wait a life time and the sound of that rock hitting earth will not reach your ears. I have never listened that long, but I have sat here, in this spot, for over an hour and never heard the rock I tossed hit the ground."

"You're sure of that." She grinned at him.

One step forward. When will I take two back?

"Yes, I am. Should I go on with my story?" He took her hand and pulled her back to sit next to him on the rock. "You are flirting with death. I don't like your infatuation with this cliff's edge. It terrifies me."

"I'm intrigued by your story and the precipice but I promise I'll stay away." She sat down with him and let him wrap his arms around her.

"The year was 1831. Eight members of the McKenna Clan, once known as the Clan Chatton, emigrated to the United States. They sailed on ships with sails as white as snow. One of the men decided to stay with the crew of the ship, and he didn't go with the rest of the group."

"What is that word, chatton?"

"It is Celtic for cat. I will tell you more about how we became known as the Chatton Clan. But for now..." Brody's pulse raced and adrenalin flowed through his veins. Almost time now for him to show her the second part...his alternate form.

"I see," she said.

Not entirely, but she would before the night ended. "Anyway, five men and two women made the journey, settling in Texas. They built houses and started businesses. But all the missing pieces did not come together. They still had unfulfilled dreams."

"Were any of those people married?" She rose and walked from him then sat down once again too close to the cliff's edge for Brody to feel comfortable.

"No, they were all single." Brody didn't know if any of this would sway Sadie to stay with him. But he knew she needed to learn everything about his life before she could make a decision.

"They all possessed the wanderlust." Sadie leaned back to look at the stars shining brightly in the sky. "I have that same longing. I want to see what is on the other side of the mountain and what is at the bottom of the cliff."

"And I wish you did not. Perhaps we could travel together." The alpha male rarely left his clan. He had been raised to lead the McKennas through this century. Carr would have to learn so much and change in too many ways to count for him to adopt the alpha male attitude and role. Carr was a playboy and a roamer, a typical second son.

Her shoulders drooped. "That would never work."

"I don't see why not."

"Because you would be unhappy. And I could not suffer that.

Sadie was right in so many ways. "Happiness would come because I was with you. But I know I would rather live here, in the Sierra Madre Mountains, in God's country."

"For a time but in the end you would return to your roots."

"Do you know me that well, Sadie Monroe?" She had nailed his emotions. He belonged here in this tiny town in the Sierra Madres, and he didn't want to live anywhere else. If one could die inside, he knew he would.

"Some things I believe I know very well. I have watched you and listened to your words. They tell me who you are."

"You sound like a profiler. My cousin Jace, does that to make his living. He profiles criminals, mostly serial killers."

"That sounds both frightening and depressing."

"I've roamed off-track. My people, they lived in Texas for a few years but as each of them found their spouses, they moved to different parts of the country, but it seemed they always moved west."

"There was more room, more land in the west." With the hint of a smile, she finished his thought for him.

"Some of the clan mated with Mexicans, Spaniards and some with people of the Native American Tribes. My ancestors ended up here, yet still many of the clan look for new horizons, continuing to wander."

"You are not one of those."

"No." He shook his head and wished he could say yes and that she didn't know him so well. But he knew if she left him, he would also die inside. So which fate was worse?

Infinity called to him, the meaning clear. She was his through all time, but she hadn't realized it yet, and he didn't know if she ever would. His heart could shatter into a million pieces.

"Chatton means cat. And the McKennas were called Clan Chatton because they have the ability to change into cats." Well, he'd blurted that out. A different way of telling her existed, he was sure.

"What? You're joking! Change into cat form?" She laughed but she wore the strangest expression on her face.

"No joke, remember your shower?" Inside his chest, his heart raced out of control. Every part of him tensed with fear at her reaction to what he was about to tell her.

"A...what part? The hot sex or the strange black cat?" Playfully, she poked at his chest. Then sat back seemingly concerned about her questions.

"The jaguar. The rosettes you have been so curious about." His voice was a soft throaty purr. His cat roaming inside his mind wanted out.

"What about him?" Her head cocked to one side, her lips thinned.

"Are you angry?"

"I'm just remembering him running off with my towel and robe. I wasn't happy about that?"

Brody couldn't help laughing out loud then he grew serious, knowing he had to tread lightly. He inhaled a long deep breath searching for the words but didn't know what to say.

"I am that cat. All jaguars have rosettes, even the black ones. They are a part of me that does not vanish when I'm in human form." The words blurted out before he had time to evaluate their impact. He could take nothing back.

"Liar, liar..."

"No," he stood, his hands on the fastenings to his jeans. "I will show you."

"You're going to strip naked. I know what that foreshadows." Sadie laughed. "This is all absurd."

"Not this time." In an instant his clothes were off. Adrenalin and a crazy energy zipped through him. Shaking, he felt the shift taking place, but was so caught up in the action, he could not see her eyes or read her expression. Blood pulsed and heated his body.

Suddenly, and on all fours he stood beside her, his tail twitching and his claws digging into the rocky earth.

"Brody!" On her feet she was backing from him, edging closer to infinity.

Terror rifled through him. She stood inches from the edge of the cliff. Rocks loosened beneath her feet. *Sadie!*

In his cat from, he could do nothing to stop her backward movement. He started to shift back just as she slipped to her knees. Groping with her hands and pushing with her feet, she found a sturdy rock to grab hold of.

"Brody, help!"

"God, Sadie." Just as it seemed she would be hurtled down the slope, he was human again.

~ * ~

I'm on a ledge—my feet." Her heart pounded. *Don't look down. Don't look down. Don't...*

"Hang on. Whatever you do, don't look down. I've shifted back. Grab me." He reached for her.

"I'm slipping—Brody!" Her toes pointed, touching the ledge, she tightened her fingers around the rocks. Then she looked up and saw Brody stretching his arms toward her. God, but she didn't want to let go of anything. Heart racing, blood pounding through her veins she saw death fly past.

Somewhere an owl hooted. A full moon hung low on the horizon and a wolf let out an eerie wail.

"Oh my, God." She looked down, waves of nausea zipped through her as her eyes blurred and the world revolved around her

Moments passed like hours as she tried to gain control of her emotions. Then as if they were detached from his body, his fingers curled around one of Sadie's wrists. With a muttered curse, he hauled her from her precarious spot.

"I've got you." Brody pulled her close, his face buried in her hair.

She was in his arms, sobbing and shaking. She felt his heart thundering against her ribs, but it wasn't as loud as hers. She needed to hang on to him forever. He was her rock, an unshakable strength.

"Brody, dear God, I've never been so terrified." Her arms wrapped so tightly around him brought her some measure of relief.

"I'm so sorry," he said, running his fingers through her hair. "I'm so sorry. But it's good now. You're safe. It's all good. I shouldn't have frightened you so. It was too much too soon."

"Hold me until I stop shaking, please." Sadie needed his warmth, wanted to feel alive. His naked body against her brought a sense of belonging. She had almost fallen to her death. She had wanted to know just how high Infinity Cliff reached into the sky, but not by falling to her death.

"I'll never stop holding you, protecting you." He drew her closer, tighter, running his hands up and down her back as if he needed to make sure she was still alive.

Sadie reciprocated, pulling Brody nearer, knowing he held the only power to stop her fear and her trembling. Needing to renew life was all she thought. Inside her, complete her, and make her whole again overpowered rational thought. She wanted Brody to make love to her, here, on top of the cliff that had nearly been her undoing.

"Brody, I want you—need you... Now."

"Are you sure?"

His question startled her. He'd always been so confident and commanding.

"Positive. Be one with me. Please."

Still naked, he stripped Sadie of her clothing. No foreplay was necessary, the moment primal and physical.

"Straddle me," he whispered.

She wrapped her legs around him. Then he was inside her. He held still for a second then stepped backward toward the rock they'd sat on earlier. With her still in his arms and his cock deep inside, he sat down. His lips melded against her and she opened for him, thrusting her tongue inside his mouth, mimicking the rhythm he set. She didn't care if Carr or Lyn were close. She knew they would turn away. If they had been nearby when she slipped over the edge, they would have raced to help.

Crying out his name and swept away with the ancient mercuric dance, Sadie shuddered again and again as the pinnacle rose to a new intense height. Harder and faster they became as one together, completing the cycle of life.

Holding her and with her legs still wrapped around him, he sat on the rocks. Stroking her hair, "I will never get enough of you, Sadie Monroe. Don't you ever leave me."

She knew in her heart, her soul would never leave his, but her body would seek out new places and different horizons. Making the most of every moment with him would be her mantra for the next few days. Every hour and every second would be blessed.

"Don't talk about that right now. I just want to feel you inside me." She closed her eyes, resting her head against his chest. Then she looked up and he captured her mouth with his.

With his teeth and tongue, he kissed her. She purred contentedly as he stroked her mouth. Her clit throbbed as once again her body was ready for him. His cock hardened inside her and pulsed. She felt the need in Brody rise. Her breath, short and raspy, "Fuck me," she whispered and felt a huge smile blossom inside and a completeness only Brody McKenna could accomplish.

"Again? Insatiable little princess. I'll do whatever you ask."

"Yes, yes, yes..."

His fingers found her clit then moved against her weeping pussy. He teased, taunted and pulled back. "Open your eyes. I want to see your eyes. I need to see the passion as I claim you."

Then he parted her further with his caress, stroking her endlessly. Surges of desire wilder than any storm came sweeping through her, and she twisted and bucked against him, moaning softly then her cries of pleasure rang out through the night. Hot liquid fire smoldered deep within her and rose until it burst inside with a myriad of emotions.

"Oh, God, Brody. I—" And then her body shuddered, trembling so intensely she couldn't breathe. Her eyes closed.

"Keep them open." His command startled her but she complied.

She scraped her nails down his back. But she didn't close her eyes until she could move no longer and her limbs were weak. "I can't." Then she let her body relax against him. "No more."

A hawk cried overhead and the loud scream of a jaguar penetrated the sultry night air.

She pressed closer to Brody, afraid of everything. "Was that a sibling?" God, but she prayed it was. "Will he come here? We've got to get dressed."

Brody laughed a long belly laugh. "Carr...he must have sensed something was wrong, that one of was in danger. No, he won't come here unless I call him." He stroked her back, ran his fingers up then down her spine. She savored the sensations, wishing she could reciprocate Brody's gentle concern and loving care.

"How would he—does he shift too?" What Brody had just showed her had shock written all over it, and if his entire family changed shape too, she was truly stunned.

"They do," he paused, waiting as if trying to gauge her reaction to his words. "My father, not my mother."

"I see. Does Nigan?" Her mind spun with all of the ramifications while she thought back to the family history Brody had just shared with her. No wonder they had left Scotland and sought out open spaces where there were no people they had to explain themselves to.

"No, but his wife shifted. She was of the clan, and he has keen senses derived from his heritage. He feels things others do not."

"Can all the children change shape?"

"It only takes one parent to continue the gene."

"So..." She wasn't sure she should go there. He had not proposed. She didn't want marriage or a family. It was too soon and she'd been adamant that she did not want a relationship of any kind. But what if all their crazy wonderful sex had accidentally... Well, she couldn't be pregnant. But they hadn't used a condom tonight.

He seemed to read her mind. "If we made a baby together, the child would be a shapeshifter."

"You know that how?" she queried, wondering if she had his child how she would deal with this strange anomaly.

"I can feel it, sense it from the depth of my soul, and remember it takes only one allele." He lifted her from his lap. "Time to get dressed."

He had stepped away from her and was now pulling on his jeans. She slipped the discarded t-shirt overhead then pulled on her pants.

"I shouldn't have asked." She had not wanted to proceed in this discussion, at least not right now.

"You had every right." He touched the tip of her nose with one finger, a sad expression on his face. "I only wish you would consider staying here—with me—as my partner in life."

She didn't want to tell him that more than once her emotional side had given in to his invitation but rational thought always prevailed.

What she did know was that she'd never been happier, never felt so free and she'd never been so protected and cherished.

"You have treated me like no other," she began. "But..." then she turned to look at the stars past the bluff she'd almost lost her life on.

"But?" He stepped in front of her and one strong finger lifted her chin. She looked into his eyes and saw the love for her shinning in their depths. Tears formed in the back of her throat.

"I don't know what to say. My heart is breaking, but I have wanted this career for a lifetime." She rubbed her arms, a chill seeping through her dousing the heat of hers and Brody's love making with a frigid coldness. "I'm not suited to be a wife or a mother. I don't know how..."

"Is there no way you can work on your own? Or bring your team here? We are of the people. From much you've told me, the Sierra Madres could be an anthropologist's dream come true. And I know from watching you there would be no better mother for a child, our child."

"I can write a proposal." The thought had already formed in her head. But the team would have to agree, and she was new to them. They were sure to go with a more established anthropologist. And they had to be approved for the grant money.

"My heart is lighter."

"That doesn't mean anything. The odds are stacked against me— us." She spoke the truth.

The sound of a horse's whinny flowed on the night wind then the sound of his hooves against the earth.

Brody pulled her farther away from the cliff then behind him. "I'm terrified for you, afraid the Chullachaqui has come for you.

Knowing this is not the devil. It was not his way. But, Sadie, you came so close to losing your life..."

"Who's there?" he called out then turned to Sadie,

"The demon slayer." The dark rider answered his question.

~ * ~

Carr let out an ear-piercing scream, his frustration at his brother tantamount to anger. Isolation and privacy were not necessary. Brody jealously guarded Sadie, and there was no reason for that emotion. Everyone in the community recognized the kinship they possessed.

"Calm down, big bro." Lyn's voice penetrated his thoughts.

"They're in trouble. I can sense it, feel it." He paced, unable to ride to his brother's rescue or shift.

"I know but... But Brody told us to stay at home. We can't let him know we disobeyed his command."

Body tensed, setting his jaw in a hard line, "He didn't believe we'd do what he said."

"Look, we have to heed his wishes. I don't feel the terror any longer. They must be safe."

"No, neither do I. It's not the devil, but something else has happened." Yet he agreed with Lyn, the terror had disappeared. Whatever had caused the fear had vanished.

"By the time we get there it might be too late to help." Lyn ran her fingers through her hair then sighed. "We could regret this but..."

"We have to go see. You lead the way. I don't think Brody will get as angry with you." Carr knew the truth. If they intruded on anything, Brody would have his hide. If they caught him naked with Sadie, better for Lyn to see than him.

"Coward."

Racing to Infinity Cliff on top his horse, he wasn't sure what deviltry was at work this night. Lyn on her horse, galloped ahead. Wind whistled through his hair. He needed to shift and run with the wind, but keeping his sanity intact was more important.

Cresting the hill, Lyn put her hand up to stop him. He reigned in with a silent curse.

"Shh..." Lyn turned to him. "They're fine. Best we wait a few minutes before we let them know we're here."

Carr's brows furrowed. "I need to see."

"No, you don't." Lyn had turned from the scene. "They're..."

"Ok, you don't have to spell it out. It's what they are always doing." Carr gave a low whistle.

"At least we're here..."

Chapter Seven

"It's dangerous out here." His speech was slow and his voice gravelly. The tone sent a shiver down Brody's spine.

Clad in black and riding a black stallion, the demon slayer rested one arm on the horn of his saddle. Tipping his hat back, he stared hard at Brody. Silence of the night engulfed them.

His square jawline and rugged features reminded Brody of a man who never settled down, one who chased sunrises. His body appeared lean and powerful, his stance intimidating a silver aura emanating from him. So still and solemn Brody wondered at his story.

"Dangerous everywhere." Brody didn't think he'd want to meet this man in a dark alley. He didn't know why, perhaps instinct, but Brody was sure the demon slayer was also a shifter.

"Seen that man over yonder, just a shadow now but he's real and treacherous." Slayer pointed behind him. "He's hunting a lady. Is that you, ma'am? If so, you need to take care."

The Slayer's question irritated Brody. At his sides his fists tightened. "Don't think that's any of your business. Maybe you should just ride on and not look back this way."

"It is if you want my help, but doesn't sound as if you do. I'm a friend." An owl cried out. Then as if in answer, a long low howl filled the silence.

To Brody the man appeared ready to unleash all the power he seemed to hold in check. "Can always use an extra pair of friendly hands." He tried to calm his breathing, but the pulse of the night set the pace. Blood surged through heated veins and the adrenalin rush was intoxicating. Brody was ready for a fight, but he needed to get Sadie somewhere safe.

"So, is the Chullachaqui after your woman?" Slayer pushed back his hat then gazed pointedly at Sadie. "She's a pretty one."

Body liked the sound of that. *My woman*. Sadie was his she just wouldn't admit it yet. But he also didn't like the way the demon slayer stared at her. "I don't know and that's the truth. We think he might be, but we don't know why. Besides, how do I know I can trust you?"

"Best you figure it out soon. He's gettin' closer. It's just a matter of time. I've been riding shotgun, and I've notice you've got a couple of friends backin' you up too. You're going to need them."

"Siblings." Brody felt the rise of anticipation. The fight would come. The only question was when. "Are they back there now?"

As if on cue, Lyn and Carr appeared over the rise, Lyn in front and Carr behind.

"What makes you think you can do a better job protecting Sadie than we can?" Carr and Lyn reigned in their horses beside Brody, while Sadie pushed in between them.

"Stop talking around me as if I'm not here." Sadie stood in front of Brody. "Thanks for your help—all of you."

"Any time, ma'am." The slayer tipped his hand and grinned. "Always itchin' for a fight when it's a good cause.

"What's your other form?" Sadie's hands were on her hips, a smile on her mouth, one toe tapping. "Seems to me it would be to everyone's advantage if we knew before the fight."

So, she thought he was a shifter too. Brody wanted to laugh out loud at her audacity. But she was right. They should know what kind of shifter he was.

"Wolf, ma'am."

"Good, it's nice to know what I might see. Don't need any more surprises tonight." Sadie let Brody encircle her with his arms. He liked the way she leaned into him, excepting his strength and protection. True enough she'd had one too many shocks.

Sadie rubbed her arms, her body shaking. He wasn't sure if she was cold or bubbling with laughter.

"You cold?" Brody didn't want any more surprises either. He needed to take away all of her demons and shield her from harm. If she were cold, the devil might be closer than anyone had thought.

"Chilled to the bone."

Brody pulled her closer. "I was hoping you were laughing. Let's get you home. Carr, Lyn you can walk with us." Fear crept through him, swallowed him whole. He knew nothing would attack them if they stayed together.

"He's close." The demon slayer looked over the landscape. "Mind if I go with you?"

"Four is better than three." Brody clasped Sadie's hand in his and began the walk down the cliff to the ranch.

Sadie poked him. "Don't I count?"

"Always, but in a fight I want you to run as fast as you can." A fight? Shit, he didn't want to chance it with Sadie around. Hell, but all he wanted was to end this--yesterday if that had been possible. Tomorrow might be a good time to search for this Chullachaqui.

"You want to meet us at sunrise?" Brody spoke to the slayer, his voice calm, resigned.

"Be a pleasure. We'll put an end to this then you won't have to worry about your woman."

Wind whistled through the canyon and a hawk soared in the dark sky above. The scent of cactus and sagebrush hovered on the air. The sun would rise in a couple of hours. When it did, Sadie would be in bed and they would be on the demon's trail.

"I'm coming with you," Sadie said.

"No fuckin' way." A shiver of apprehension and dread swept down Brody's spine. He had to be able to trust her to stay where he knew she wasn't in harm's way.

"Staying at your gramps home is not an option. I don't feel safe by myself." Sadie's hands fisted. "I don't feel safe anywhere you aren't."

"You'll be protected there." Brody persisted but he wasn't sure how. His great grandfather was old and no longer the powerful man he once was.

"At least leave your sister with me for some protection."

Brody turned to Lyn. "What do you think?"

"She has a good point," Lyn said. "Oh my god!"

The earth shook and rumbled. Below them boulder size rocks crashed down to the valley floor. The air around them thundered.

"Don't move." Brody shouted. His heart in his throat and his body frozen, seconds passed before he grabbed Sadie's hand. The shaking and rumbling stopped. Earth and wind stilled. Calmness surrounded them in direct opposition to the chaos that had enclosed them a moment before.

"What the hell just happened?" Sadie clung to Brody.

"Earthquake."

Fear pummeling through him, he tried to see below but debris littered the landscape. And even if it wasn't so dark, he could not have seen the ranch.

"Gramps." Fear enveloped Brody. "We need to get back to the ranch. He tugged Sadie until they raced down the cliff. But she couldn't keep up with him. Lyn and Carr shifted and outpaced everyone. Their horses had bolted for home.

"Go with them. I will see to your woman." Slayer stopped his horse and waited.

Brody's heart froze, second thoughts foremost in his head. He didn't want to leave her but he needed to trust. Trust for Brody had often been elusive. He looked to the slayer, breath stopped, nerves frayed.

He couldn't help but look at Sadie for assistance, hoping she would help him decide.

As if reading his mind, Sadie nodded toward the ranch, "Go on, I'm fine. No chills. Slayer will make sure I get there safe."

Relieved she understood what he wanted to know, "You sure?"

"Yes. Go on, do what you need to do." She leaned in and kissed him on the cheek.

"She needs to ride." Slayer leaned down from his horse. "Give me your hand. We will meet them."

"Do it." Brody knew he had to get to the ranch. The sick feeling in his gut would not disappear.

Sadie reached out her hand and with the help of Slayer, she swung onto the horse.

Brody shifted, clothes shredded and the wind whipped them away. He sprang forward, racing down the cliffs to his gramps home. He didn't know what he would find there, and he prayed his grandfather was safe.

~ * ~

Strength and power emanated from Slayer. In one swift move, he'd pulled her onto the horse and behind him. When Brody shifted, she felt overwhelming emotions sweep inside. The incredible sight left her breathless. In his cat form, Brody was magnificent.

Powerful.

Sadie no longer had time to think.

"Hang on," Slayer kicked his horse into a trot then turned him onto a different path. Boulders as well as lose gravel littered the trail. The animals chattered as if relaying a message.

"Where are you going?" Her certainty that Slayer was not the demon wavered. Her breath caught in her throat.

"We cannot take the same trail as the great cats." Slayer fell silent. "They run with limitless agility. This horse would break a leg if we followed in their path."

His words were true. The horse could not follow. They had to find a different way to the valley below. Time was of the essence but arriving there more important.

"I am not the Chullachaqui."

"I know." The assurance in her words and the determination to trust felt right. She clung to him, closing her eyes and listening to the steady beat of the horse's hooves. She tuned into her senses, felt the light breeze across her face and the scent of sage.

"Then why fear me?" Slayer spoke in a quiet tone, but the question was relevant. In ways she did fear him.

"You are the unknown." She had felt the cold but this man was not the demon. She knew his warmth and his sincerity. "I have always been hesitant around those who are new to me."

Except Brody... That thought took her by surprise.

"Hang on."

They had reached a wide flat trail. Slayer kicked the horse into a gallop. She couldn't help but cling to him. Her hair flew behind her and her nails bored into the man in front of her. She leaned her head against his back to keep the wind from her eyes. The ride exhilarated. When she and Brody rode to the ranch, they never pushed the horses any harder than an easy trot, and that only one time.

No, Slayer was not evil. So close to him, she knew she would feel the cold emanate from him. Next to her, his body was warm and vibrant. Vibrations of his laughter sprang from his chest.

"I trust you." For a second her voice fluttered then she felt reassured with her words. "I do...trust."

"It's about time, little one." Slayer's gravelly voice was filled with laughter.

"I don't understand." She moved away from him, leaving a sliver of space. She saw the simmering silver glow around him and wondered at the sight. "You are different from them."

"In time you will comprehend." He pointed toward the ranch. "See, we are almost there. You will be safe and we will kill the demon for you."

Sadie closed her eyes and recalled everything Slayer told her. She wanted facts and the whys about things. Dealing in the abstract was not something she appreciated. *In time...*

"So you can see into the future?" Skeptical of his words, Sadie wanted to explore them in depth.

Laughter rumbled from his chest. "You are too inquisitive. Curiosity can get you into deep trouble."

"I'll walk the rest of the way." Sadie prodded him on the back with a finger. The knot in her stomach had disappeared, but she wasn't sure about the swaying horse.

"No, I promised your man I would keep you safe. I mean to deliver you to him personally. All of the anger you have pent up inside for me can best be used in a positive way."

Sadie paused a moment in thought. She wasn't angry. She wasn't sure how she felt. "You have a name?"

"Angel."

Laughter bubbled up inside. "You are the farthest from the image of an angel I have ever had."

"The name reflects my personality." He nickered to his horse. "My mount believes me an angel every time I feed him and brush him down."

"Of course he would."

"And do you have a last name?" Curiosity drove her questions. She was sure she heard him swallow hard and knew it wasn't something he wanted to reveal. Again intrigue seemed to follow this man.

The pause was long and vibrated with tension. "McKenna."

"O—kay." She wasn't at all sure about this. Angel shifted to a wolf. What was with that? McKennas shifted to jaguars. She could understand if it was a lion or a tiger but a wolf?

He didn't wait for her to ask. "I don't know the answer to that question in your head. Maybe a genetic malfunction." Angel shrugged. "But my closest relatives all shift to wolf form."

"Is that possible?"

"We are here." Angel helped her dismount. "It must be. I and my family are living proof."

"Brody." Sadie stepped up beside him, his arm out stretched to pull her into his embrace. "Is Nigan okay?"

"Yes, but the house received major damage. When we arrived, we had to pull Gramps from beneath the wreckage. A bookcase fell on him. His pride was hurt more than his body. Lyn is seeing to his needs."

"When will you go?" She shuddered at the thought of Brody fighting the Amazonian devil. If it weren't for the McKennas, she'd probably be the devil's prize by now.

"Soon..." Brody looked to the horizon. The sun was rising and the sky was mottled with colors. "Don't be afraid."

"You read my mind. I'm terrified for you and your brother. I hope you find him and can bring him in."

Brody roughed back his hair then cleared his throat. "This probably won't end with an arrest. He has to die or he'll keep coming after you. I won't have that constant fear hanging over your head."

Sadie shivered as a chill swept up her spine. Death was what Brody meant. Someone would die. "I don't like the sound of that. I don't want to see any of you hurt because of me." Feelings of guilt swept through Sadie. A tear slid down her cheek.

"The demon wants you, no one else. He's not going to give up, and even if we did bring him in, I doubt if a jail cell would hold him very long." Brody touched the drop of moisture with the tip of his finger.

"It's a fight to the finish. But we are four now and he is only one," Carr said.

She wondered if the demon understood that? Trickery and subterfuge would have to be dealt with.

~ * ~

Akando stood on a cliff above the ranch, watching the McKennas gather together and work as one to clear the debris. He didn't like the feelings in his gut. This did not bode well for him. There were four shifters now. He would have to find a way to separate them. It was the only way he'd be successful.

Divide and conquer. I am an Amazonian devil, Chullachaqui. She is my destiny.

"I'm going home." Celinda paced the cliff, a frown marring her features. "There is nothing for either of us here. They will kill you."

Akando waved a hand in the air. "I'm dead if I don't get the woman. I will never give up." He wouldn't quit trying to have her. He didn't care how long it took. There would come a time when the McKenna would let down his guard. And it would only take one time.

"I'm dead if I stay with you. I'm not going to let that tramp end my life." Celinda looked to the south, toward her homeland.

Akando shrugged, not caring what the woman did. "Suit yourself." He tossed a rock into the air just to hear it fall.

Falling...

He'd nearly raced to Infinity Cliff when he'd watched Sadie slip over the cliff. She could have fallen to her death, and he wouldn't have been able to save her. Stupid shifter had to show off for her. Look what it almost caused.

"I will."

"When are you leaving?" Akando didn't think it would be soon enough.

Celinda gave him a frosty glare. "Tonight."

So that was the game she played. "You want me to talk you into staying?

"No, I want you to talk yourself into leaving. If you stay, you're going to die here. I've seen it and felt it. Leave with me while you still have a choice."

Chapter Eight

Brody pulled Sadie into his arms. Her warmth engulfed him, penetrated the frigid chill and the black omen of his thoughts. Good god, but he wanted the events from the past week to be over, to vanish, needed to know she would be safe from this devil.

He closed his eyes as he felt her face against his chest, holding her there with his hands. She was so tiny and so fragile. He didn't want to leave her here, unprotected except by Lyn. But there was no other choice.

"It will all be fine." She looked up her eyes sparkling with tears then she traced the seam of his lips with one delicate finger.

"Do you really believe that, Sadie?" If anything happened to her, nothing would be okay. His life would end. A myriad of emotions ripped him apart.

"Of course." But her voice held little conviction and her trembling shoulders did little to alleviate his fears. "Lyn will be here, Nigan and all of his people. I promise he won't be able to lure me away."

"Don't be afraid for any of us. Angel, Carr and myself, we know how to take care of ourselves and will return to you." Brody's attempt to reassure was weak and halfhearted. Not because he was afraid for any of them, but he was terrified that somehow the beast would capture Sadie. But he hoped she listened. The Chullachaqui would be vanquished.

"I can't help the terror. After you walk over that hill, I won't know what is happening." Sadie reached behind his head and tugged at him until their lips met in a soft kiss. Her lips melded with his, begging for entrance.

Brody ran his hands up her spine. Because of the days of travel, she had lost weight. A surge of guilt whipped through him, but the moment was forgotten. The kiss sent his mind spinning and his inner cat purring. Her tongue swept his mouth. When he opened for her, their tongues danced and played in a way older than time, primal. His heart thundered beneath his ribs and rushing blood set his body on fire.

With his tongue, he traced her teeth then pushed inside, knowing she wanted more and understanding how much he needed her. It was more than erotic, more than sexual and she was so much more than a good fuck. Sadie was the part of him that had been missing for so long. He guessed she had dark secrets, and he knew he needed to find a way to purge her mind of them and convince her there was light, and he was the light she needed.

"Come on, Brody, you can have all the time you want with her when we get back." Carr's voice reverberated in Brody's head, but he pushed it back then glowered at his brother. He had nothing to say to that except words he wouldn't be able to take back.

He pulled her close, reveling in the feel of her breasts against him, of her tongue mating with his and the throaty purrs coming from deep inside her throat. And he chased Carr's words from his head.

She pulled away, pushing her hair from her face then running her hands along her arms. "You should go. The sooner this is over the sooner I will find a measure of peace."

"Wait here and don't do anything foolish," Brody told her, his mind racing with all the possible scenarios. Perhaps he should send Carr and Angel after the devil and he should stay and guard Sadie.

"I promise." She smiled at him then set her hand against his chest, her fingers spreading over his heart.

"You 'bout done?" Carr pushed his hat back from his forehead and appeared as impatient as hell. "The rest of us are waiting. Or are you afraid of the dreaded Amazonian devil?"

"None of your business, little bro. And you know I'm not afraid to fight the devil." *But I'm terrified for Sadie and Lyn.*

"It is when I'm putting my life in danger for you." Carr tapped his gloved hands against the sides of his legs.

Angel chuckled as he crossed his arms over his chest. "Don't start the fight here. Need to conserve energy."

"Lyn, don't let her out of your sight." Brody strode toward his horse, his nerves ragged as hell.

"Will do." Lyn acted as if that was a no brainer. She walked closer to Sadie. "We'll be connected at the hip."

Brody walked back and touched Sadie's cheek with the back of his hand. "I'll be done with the devil in no time at all. Stay in the house and with Lyn. We don't know what this guy is up to except he wants you. And the only way he can get to Sadie Monroe is to entice you away. Remember that. He will stop at nothing, disguise himself as one of us..."

"I'll be here and safe. I'm not going to leave the house for any reason."

A few seconds later the men were mounted and cantering away from the ranch. Brody looked back to see Sadie and Lyn watching them. Fear balled in his gut. Something didn't bode well, but he couldn't quite figure out what was wrong.

Instinct told him to turn back.

Duty kept him riding.

"You seem a bit distant. What's wrong?" Angel asked.

"Don't like the feelings swimmin' in my gut." Brody looked back to the ranch once more.

"You can stay here." Carr raised an eyebrow as if he understood Brody's apprehension.

"No, deep down I think the danger is out there, not lurking by the ranch. I pray I'm right."

"Any time... If you change your mind, turn and ride back. No explanations are needed," Angel said.

"Any time I change my mind?" Brody knew he should be with Sadie, but he wasn't ready to leave these men, his brother and new friend, to fight this devil by themselves. Minutes ticked by and they seemed like hours, yet still they rode.

Miles from the ranch Brody inhaled the wind and caught no scent. The air was clean and hot. The wind was alive with songs of birds and animals--but not the Chullachaqui.

"Yeah, I don't smell anything either." Carr looked to his brother for confirmation.

Angel gave it instead. "We're going the wrong way."

In unison they turned their horses and headed back to the ranch. They'd traveled far and time now was important.

Fear for Sadie, his sweet Sadie, pooled in his gut. Horse hooves pounded the earth, yet he couldn't go fast enough. Landscape blurred; rocks, cliffs, trees, grass all became one. His inner cat prowled through his head, wanting to free itself.

Save Sadie.

Save her.

Reach her before the spawn of the devil tempts her to the dark side where she would never be able to return.

The scent came to him on the wind, filled his senses with dread. Seconds turned to minutes as his heart thundered beneath his ribs. Chills swept through him, his breath stilled.

"Calm yourself, big bro." The words were spoken in his mind. Carr talked to him—reassured him. He knew the need to stay in control was imperative. But the need to act overpowered all senses. So torn, he couldn't think straight, Brody tried to follow Carr's lead.

For a moment Brody closed his eyes and became one with the horse, the wind and the sun. Golden beams of courage swept through him. Fear for Sadie evaporated like a spring rain.

"I will try."

"If you are to save her, you must do more than try."

"I understand." And he did, but understanding and accomplishing the feat were different.

As they neared the ranch, they reined in then stopped. The air stilled, the rancid, scent permeating the chill of the day was wicked. Pain stabbed him and his gut churned. Evil penetrated.

Brody swallowed hard as he scanned the terrain for any sign of Sadie. A dangerous calm, instinctive in an animal about to kill, swept through his body. Every muscle tightened and became one with his mind. Deep in his throat, he growled, low and menacing.

Sadie stood atop a hill. Sunbeams surrounded her, casting her body in an eerie glow. She was motionless for a few seconds then she raised her arms into the air and walked forward, toward the Amazonian devil.

"No..." Brody's anguished cry ripped through the world as he watched his mate move closer to the devil.

~ * ~

Emptiness filled Sadie's heart as she saw the men disappear along the horizon. Coldness washed over her. "God, I hope nothing happens to them. I don't think I could live with myself if..."

"Nothings going to happen. They are strong and they are three. He is only one. Come on, let's go into the house and get something to eat. I'll bet you're as hungry as I am." Lyn started off to the ranch then looked over her shoulder at Sadie. "Come on."

"I don't like waiting." Sadie remembered all the days she and her father had waited for her mother to return. But she never did. She never phoned or wrote. Her dad moved on but her mom's actions sat heavy on Sadie's heart, molding her into who she was today.

"Neither do I, girlfriend. Neither do I. But it will be easier on a full stomach. I'm famished." Lyn headed back to the ranch with Sadie following.

"If you don't mind, I'd like to be alone. I've work and a few notes to make in my journal. I'll eat later." Yes, her journal notes. How long had it been since she'd written in it? It was at the hot springs and she'd known then she was half in love with Brody. But she'd also known she wasn't about to let anything materialize from her infatuation.

"All right, but I promised not to leave you by yourself. If you want to go anywhere, let me know. Stay in your room. You hear me? I've got a meeting with some eggs and bacon."

"Scout's honor." Sadie stepped ahead of Lyn and made her way to the room she and Brody shared. Lyn stayed two steps behind her, and when Sadie shut the door, she guessed Lyn settled down outside. She felt a tad guilty about keeping Lyn from her food, but a few moments later she heard Lyn ordering her breakfast.

The action reminded her of Carr standing guard outside her room the first night she'd met Brody. And the first time they'd made love.

Inside she rummaged through her backpack. Notebooks and pencils were what she was after. When Brody told her she could not take her computer, he provided writing material. She found a week-old candy bar, which she devoured. Then she sat down to begin writing.

Dear journal,

"Everything ok?" Lyn's voice rang out startling Sadie. "You're so quiet. I was getting worried."

"I'm fine." Sadie stopped writing and stretched out the kinks along her spine. She wasn't used to spending so much time on top of a horse. Her legs and her back were sore. Now that she thought about it, every part of her hurt.

"If you need anything, just holler."

Sadie opened the door with laughter in her voice. "Cause you're not going anywhere, right?"

"I made a promise and I aim to be keepin' it."

"Umm...what's that I smell?" Sadie's stomach grumbled. She hadn't eaten since a light snack the day before. Until this moment she hadn't realized how hungry she was.

"Bacon, eggs and potatoes. Want some? I ordered it up a few minutes ago. Seems as if cook anticipated our hunger. She had already made it, enough for everyone." Lyn stood outside the door, breakfast tray in hand a huge frown plastered on her face. "I really could use some company, if you don't mind. Don't mean to be selfish but...

Lyn set the tray on the desk in the small bedroom then stepped back with a look of anticipation and worry.

"You really didn't have to cook for me."

"No problem. As I said, Cook did all the work. I'm just the delivery girl and I was hungry too." Lyn piled her plate high.

Sadie watched, feeling for the first time in her life as if she belonged. "Thank you," she said between mouthfuls of eggs and potatoes.

"So...what are you working on? Brody said you were an anthropologist." Lyn leaned forward and fingered through some of her papers. "Never quite understood the profession. Seems a bit strange to me."

"A...those are personal, just a hopeful budding anthropologist. I'm here to write a proposal for a research project. My team spread out up and down the U.S. and when we get together in a couple of weeks we'll decide which project to take on. These are really good."

"You'll be leaving here? Brody's not going to like that." Lyn forked more eggs into her mouth then chewed, watching Sadie this time, a look of curiosity resting on her face.

"I don't know why. We don't have any commitments to each other." Sadie understood what Lyn said. Brody had made it clear he didn't want her to leave, and she'd told him she was going.

"Brody believes in his heart that you belong to him and he to you. It's the way of our kind. He won't part with your company without putting up a fight." Lyn picked up a notebook. "Butterflies. Why...why would you leave a man who clearly adores you?"

"I don't know that he adores me." Sadie picked at her food, her hunger vanishing. She had thought she would never be faced with this type of situation. "Leaving might be hard, but he'll get over it and probably move on in a matter of days. And the butterfly migration can tell us something about the migration of the people—your people."

"In that you're wrong—about Brody getting over you." Lyn picked up the dishes then settled them on the tray. "I'll take the tray to the kitchen. Don't go anywhere. We can talk some more about this. I'll be back as soon as I clean up the cooking mess."

"Where would I go?"

Sadie sat back down with her journal.

I've never felt so disjointed in my life and so full of questions. I no longer know or understand what exactly it is that I want from my future. I know I don't want to fall in love and have that person leave me. I don't want to spend a lifetime waiting for them to poke their head inside my door and pick up a relationship that never really began.

God, but I know what I don't want, but what is it that I want?

Sadie set the notebook down and let the pencil slide from her fingers. The light tap as it hit the ground startled Sadie from her musings.

What is it I want? Not a lifetime in the back hills of the Sierra Madre Mountains barefoot and pregnant. But Sadie knew her life wouldn't have to be that way. It could be what she made of it. Brody would give her that option.

Sadie peered out the window, her gaze settling on a form walking at the top of the hill. The men had disappeared hours ago. As the form moved closer, she realized it was a man and he walked with a limp. He stopped and wiped his brow then stared hard in her direction. It seemed to Sadie he knew she watched.

"Brody?" God, the man looked like him and he was hurt. She wasn't supposed to go anywhere without Lyn. But if that was Brody, she had to help him. If anything happened to him and she didn't go to him, she would never forgive herself. She looked to the door then back to the hillside.

"Please understand, Lyn. Please..."

Sadie grabbed her first aid kit and slipped through the open window. The sun beat down and the air stilled. Brody stopped when he saw Sadie. He waved at her but she wasn't sure what he tried to tell her. It appeared he motioned for her to come to him.

Caution was supposed to be the name of the game, but she wanted to race the wind to reach his side faster.

He can change into any form. You'll know it's the Chullachaqui because you'll feel cold.

I don't feel cold or chilled.

Her stiff spine and wavering emotions would make it harder to climb the hill to Brody, but she couldn't relax. An inner voice cried out restraint. Her stomach churned in trepidation. The closer she walked, the more determined she became to discover the truth. Cold settled slowly into her core. When she tried to stop and turn around, she couldn't.

No...

This wasn't supposed to happen. Face to face with the devil, she felt helpless to defend herself. He had won and she could do nothing to stop. The scent of rotting flesh assailed her.

"My, my Sadie, we finally meet." A devil's grin crossed his face and the smile showed rotting brown teeth. His stench made her retch.

"I'm not your Sadie." Lifting her face and wiping her mouth, she was surprised she could speak or breathe then she pulled on an inner strength. A strength derived from her time with Brody. A fierce hatred for this horrible being rooted in her head.

"Oh, but you will be. Soon, Sadie, soon." He touched her cheek and she tried to flinch away, but the coldness seemed to have frozen the movement. She found she couldn't move, couldn't walk or run from this demon. But he hadn't won, he couldn't. Brody would save her.

"Never."

Diabolical laughter emanated from him as he threw his head

back. "I love your courage, your feisty nature. The first time I saw you in Peru, I knew you would be mine."

"Peru?"

"My dear, we will have time to discuss all the details of this later. Now I must get us out of here." He reached for her hand. Their fingers touched. Ice filled her veins. Her mind cried out her stupidity.

"I won't..."

"You have no choice."

Like a zombie she walked with the devil incarnate. Seconds passed as hours. One step, two steps, yet eternity faded into nothingness. Grass gave way to rocky path.

The wild screech penetrated her mind. She stopped, motionless and watched the devil shift into a sleek jaguar. The cat whirled then faced its attacker.

"Ghost..." demon said.

A beautiful albino cat leapt for the devil's juggler. The devil fought the other cat off, pushing it away with huge paws and leaving a streak of blood across the albino cats back.

"Lyn...? My god, no."

With the loss of focus, the devil's control of her mind faded. Coldness no longer penetrated her soul and her body. Sadie knew she should run, but she didn't want to leave Lyn to fend for herself.

Stupid girl, what could she do?

Run...

Sadie felt warmth slide into her hands and feet. Her core strengthened and her mind grew strong. With one last look at her friend and the courageous fight going on in front of her, Sadie fled.

At the bottom of the path, she stopped. A cry of pain seared the afternoon sky and floated upward. Then the sound of pounding horse hooves flew through air. She watched Carr slide off his horse and shift,

Angel did the same as they rushed to Lyn's defense.

"Sadie..." Brody cried out her name. The anguish filled her to the core. She had done just what she was not supposed to do, and she'd put Lyn's life in danger because of her mistake. But she'd thought...

"Brody. I'm so sorry. I'm so very sorry." He swept her onto his horse. She sat behind him, her arms around his body. And she clung to him with a quiet desperation.

"Hush, it's okay."

Angel in his wolf form and Carr in his cat form charged up the hill where Lyn had fought a courageous battle. Lyn lay battered on the ground, blood pooling on the ground around her. The devil tried to flee but Angel leapt upon him and sunk his teeth in Akando's neck. Tail twitching and claws ready, Carr blocked his path.

The battle raged while Lyn lay motionless on the ground. Fur and blood flew through the air. Screeches of pain and furry filled the afternoon sky.

Then a death cry rolled across the battered earth.

The jaguar screamed and the wolf let out a long howl.

Chapter Nine

Sadie's body shook with a fierceness she couldn't understand. The trembling wasn't from the cold but from fear, and the terror that Lyn might die because of her stupidity. Despite the warnings and the knowledge, she walked into the devil's arms.

How many times had she been told not to leave the ranch? An unvoiced explicative flew in her mind.

How many times had Lyn promised to protect her? Now Lyn might have paid the ultimate price for that undertaking.

Her life.

"It's going to be all right." Brody's assurance did nothing to make her feel better. She didn't want to open her eyes and look up the hill. She didn't want to see Lyn's lifeless body.

"You don't know that. It was my fault. Her cat form is so beautiful. I've never seen...she is one of a kind, isn't she?"

Brody stroked her hair then turned her face to meet his gaze. "Open your eyes, sweet Sadie. Lyn isn't dead. The Chullachaqui is. Nigan will see to Lyn and she will heal. Soon she will be back to her feisty little self. And yes, albinos are rare in any animal."

Sadie did as Brody requested. What she saw made her heart stop. Carr carried Lyn's limp body. Still in her cat form, she appeared lifeless. "Is she going to be all right?" She wanted to beat her fists against Brody's chest until she had no more energy, and she needed to see into the future.

"I told you, she will be fine." Brody pulled her close. "You are warmer now. I'm glad."

He should be asking her why she had been a reckless fool. Why she'd put Lyn in danger. Instead, he tried to soothe her shattered emotions. "Lyn doesn't look fine. She's not moving. I can't see her breathe. And the blood, why is there so much? That should be me, not Lyn."

"We can have this argument until doom's day. As a shifter, I know things that cannot be explained. Believe me, please. You don't need to worry. Carr will take her to gramp's healing lodge and when the two of them emerge, Lyn will be well and just as cocky as she has always been. Don't say it should be you who is injured. Don't ever say or think that again."

"Carr, he's naked." Sadie nodded in Carr's direction. "He..."

"That's the thing about shifting. It wreaks havoc on clothing if one doesn't have time to disrobe. We were a bit pressed, it seems. Good thing Lyn is covering him." Brody let out a chuckle, amused at his brother's look of chagrin when he noticed they watched.

Angel had remained in his wolf form and trotted beside Carr. He stopped for a second and sniffed the wind then he sat back on his haunches and let loose a howl that sent shivers down Sadie's spine. A few moments later Angel raced away.

"Going to get some clothes." With a bellowing laugh, Brody moved in the saddle and pulled Sadie's arms around his waist.

"Will he...will Angel leave? I'd like a chance to thank him for everything he's done." Tears filled her eyes then slipped down her cheeks.

"Don't know. I'm going to get you back to the house and bring Carr something to wear. He won't want to let Lyn go until he can hand her over to gramps. And he's probably feeling uncomfortable right now."

"Why hasn't Lyn shifted?" Sadie's head rested against Carr's back. It was all she could do to stay on the horse, she was so exhausted. But she'd sensed a need to change the subject, and she didn't want to rest until she knew Lyn's fate.

"She's hurt too bad. A lot of energy is involved when shifting. Right now all of Lyn's body is working on healing. She's not physically capable of changing form. She'll stay in cat form until her body has the strength it needs."

Brody's reply surprised Sadie. She wanted to poke Brody in the chest and demand the truth and answers he seemed to be withholding then wipe the day away from her memories. Erasing what happened here from her head would be a formidable task indeed. "You told me a few minutes ago she was going to be fine."

"Her injuries need tending, but they are not life threatening. As I said a moment ago, right now she doesn't have enough strength to return to her human form. She must rest until her powers are stronger."

Brody would never understand the guilt she felt and the terror that had purged her heart when she saw Lyn go down. "Can I see her?"

"Gramps will stand vigil after he applies the right herbs to the wounds. When she wakes up, you can go see her." Brody's patience astounded her. He was so calm and controlled.

They reached the house. Brody dismounted then helped Sadie. "Thank you. I will try to understand."

Gramps was beside them, holding out a pair of jeans and a black t-shirt. "For Carr? You read my mind."

"No, I saw..." the elder said with a chuckle in his voice. Then he turned to Sadie, "Lyn will heal. Now you must rest."

"Will you get Sadie to our room?"

Nigan nodded then slanted Sadie a look that seemed to say. "Can't she find her own way?"

"I won't go anywhere. I promise and this time I'll keep that promise. I have writing left unfinished." Her journal had fallen to the floor left open, and she wanted to add to it, spill out her heart.

"All right then, I'll be back in a few minutes with Lyn and Carr." The tenderness in his voice resonated to her core.

"Hurry." She watched him turn his horse then kick it to a gallop.

A few seconds later Lyn was atop the horse, settled behind Brody like a big sack of grain. Carr had dressed and walked beside the two, keeping one hand on Lyn's back.

When they reached the house, the men helped take Lyn to the place of healing, a small hut at the side of the ranch house.

"Thought you were going to our room." He slanted and eyebrow and seemed to watch her with a strange expression on his face. Yet his sensitivity was a feeling she'd remember forever.

"I was but I couldn't tear my eyes away from watching you. I'm so afraid for Lyn. I want to sit by her and pray. I need to apologize for being so incredibly stupid and for putting her in danger." Sadie wiped the moisture from her cheek.

"Gramps will see to her. She doesn't need us right now. But I know I want you." Brody winked then laughed. "I think you know exactly what I'm feelin'."

Sadie rubbed her arms, "I don't know. My skin feels as if all kinds of bugs and things are crawling on them. I can't shake his smell or rid myself of the feel of his touch."

One perfectly sculpted Brody eyebrow rose a fraction of an inch.

"Let's take a shower. The water and my attentions will rid you of the feel of creepy crawly bugs."

Sadie knew what he meant. The feeling of water against her flesh might assuage the guilt she felt. But nothing would vanquish the fact that Lyn could die because of her stupidity. "Okay. Maybe you're right." The thought of Brody and the shower was not enough to make her feel better. Yet she was willing to try.

"I'll race you..."

"What." Brody flew past her and into the house. She laughed and let out a screech. "Cheater!"

She raced behind him, knowing she couldn't catch him then lost her breath when she rounded the corner before their room. He stepped in front of her and scooped her into his arms then twirled her.

"I'd never cheat." His whispered words next to her ear sent shivers of warmth sprinting through her to her core. "I want to help you forget."

She pounded his chest as her body resonated with need. "You know you would."

"If it means I would hold onto you forever, yes I would." His teeth found her earlobe and bit gently down. Then he let his tongue explore it. He placed gentle kisses down her neck and across her collarbone.

"Brody."

"What?" His angelic sounding voice made her giggle. "See, I'm making you feel better. Just think how you'll feel when I'm finished."

"Like a limp noodle. Put me down. We need to get clean clothes." She pushed on him but his mouth molded over hers. His tongue plunged inside, dancing a magical melody deep within hers.

"Do I have to?" He purred deep in the back of his throat. "I never want to let you go."

"Yes." Sadie understood the cat-like sound and need to hear more from him. But she held on tight, wrapping her arms around him and running her hands through his hair. Then she responded to his kiss, her tongue mating with his.

"I don't want to but I'd rather get to the shower." He complied, setting her on the floor then leaning against the doorframe of their room and watched her gather belongings for herself; a blouse, shorts, sandals.

"Aren't you going to get clean clothes?"

"I'd rather watch you." But he stepped forward and in a few seconds had a stack of items.

"I thought this was a race." Sadie slipped past him and around the corner. She heard him laugh then his feet pounding on the floor.

Breathless, she leaned against the wall of the shower. Her towel and clothes draped where they wouldn't get wet. She never would grow tired of looking at Brody McKenna. His broad shoulders, lean body with ripped abs, captivated her every sense. The faint rosettes on his body were meant for tracing with a fingertip.

"God, you're beautiful." She stepped forward then touched his chest and ran a finger around the rosette she'd just admired.

His breath inhaled was swift and deep. "I'm supposed to tell you that, sweet Sadie."

"You can—every minute of every day." At least the ones we have left.

"You're beyond beautiful if that's possible." Reaching out, he slipped a lock of hair behind her ear. "I want you."

"I know." Sadie slipped her shirt over her head, letting it drop at her feet. She needed to touch him, but he held her hands away from him.

He turned her and unhooked her bra.

"Sadie, sweet sexy Sadie. For today, for this moment, you are mine." He brushed her nipples with the palms of his hands, his dark sooty lashes covering his eyes as he stared downward. Running his fingers around her nipples, she shuddered against him. Her core clenched and pulsed with need.

She let her forehead fall against his chest. "Brody..."

Then his hands found the fastenings of her jeans. In seconds they were on the floor along with her panties. His clothes followed then he turned on the shower.

"Wash first, cleanse all thoughts of the devil from your soul." Brody lathered his hands with soap and washed her from her neck to her toes, not missing one spot, the process more erotic and enticing than any foreplay.

"God, Brody, this is torture."

"No, pleasure."

"But my body is in grave need. I want you inside me. Now." Sadie grabbed the soap form Brody's hands then lathered him everywhere. His purr of pleasure delighted her.

On her knees she touched his cock, washed and rinsed it then traced it's length with her tongue. "Do you like this?"

"Oh, fuck."

Then his cock was inside her mouth. She sucked, her teeth gently moving up and down.

"I wanted this to be slow." He came inside her mouth.

~ * ~

His body shook with the explosion of cum. A moment later he pulled her up, her breasts against his chest. "Dear God, Sadie. What you do to me." He needed her by his side for the rest of his life.

She wrapped her arms around him. "No. What you do to me. I cannot resist your charms, Brody McKenna."

His laughter lightened his mood. "Oh, yes, what I'm about to do to you. Can you imagine what it is?"

"Show me," Sadie's purr mimicked Brody's. The delight he felt could not be measured.

He ran his hands down to her butt and squeezed then pulled against his hardened cock. He had to laugh at himself. Getting enough of Sadie Monroe would never happen. She was his life, his soul and his heart.

"I'm waiting." She wiggled against him, taunting and encouraging him.

"Little minx." He ran his tongue around the shell of her ear, loving the way she tasted as well as the feel of her silken flesh.

"I need you inside. I want to feel whole again. I mean to purge thoughts of the Amazonian devil from my head."

"I'm not going to let you rush me. No, I think I will paint a picture with words." Brody knew this would not be slow, but he meant to take as much time as his body as well as hers would allow. Already hard and pulsing with need, he gritted his teeth, trying for more time.

"Even though you won't admit it, you are a nurturer. If you had a child, the babe would want for nothing. Would you ever consider a child with me?" He touched her rose colored nipple then placed his hand where he felt the steady beat of her pulse.

"My plans...I would be a terrible mother."

"You have a heart of gold and a will of iron. Yet when I thought you had fallen off that cliff, a part of me died. You want to take on the world, but I'm afraid you will put yourself in such danger..." The danger she'd already encountered sent terror through his head. If he couldn't be her protector through life, he would die inside.

In his gut he knew no one had spoken to Sadie this way. No one, not her parents or anyone else, had faith in her or feared for her the way he did. Her parents had abused her in ways she'd never spoken of, but he knew they had robbed her of childhood she could never retrieve.

"I don't know what to say." She looked at him with a stubborn pride and innocent eyes.

He bent and captured one nipple between his teeth. His body, rock-hard, wanted Sadie in the most primal way. Every muscle tightened as he tried to hold back and make this mating perfect for her. They'd always climaxed so fast. Inwardly, he grinned. She was ready for him. Now.

Touching her clit then slipping one finger inside, he was met with cream. "Say you want me."

"God, is there any question?" She moved, her body quivering as if on the precipice.

"Say you want me." Brody meant to persist in this.

"Brody?"

"Say you want me." His finger slipped inside then back out.

"I want you." Her voice quavered as she spoke.

"Ok good, wrap your legs around me. Wait."

"I can't wait. You make me tell you I want you then you say wait?"

"I have to get protection."

She stepped back and watched as he slipped on the condom. He remembered a time not to long ago he'd forgotten the protection. For himself, he didn't care if she were pregnant with his child. But he knew it was too soon for her. She had plans and he had spent many an hour in thought as to how he could help her facilitate her plans.

He finished. She jumped up, wrapping her legs around him. He was inside her just as fast. Pinned next to the shower wall, he tried to hold back and fought to keep the pace slow. Overcome with need, he lost all patience. She moved against him until she shook with such violence he exploded inside. The force of her climax overwhelmed him.

"I cannot breathe. I think my heart has stopped. I feel as if I've run a marathon and in record time." She let her head rest against his shoulder. The tempo and shaking of her body continued as he massaged the muscles of her back.

"Come. Let's try this again, foreplay before the sex. Maybe I can succeed where I've failed before." He set her down then poured soap into the palm of his hand. Then with a wicked grin, he soaped her down, taking delight in her body, running his hands over every part of her then rinsing her with the warm water.

"My turn." Sadie did the same.

He groaned when she washed him. "My god." He pulled her against him. His finger on her clit he worked it until she was shaking against him in climax. Their mouths joined, tongues mating.

Later they were exhausted yet replenished. Dressed, they found their way to the healing tent to see Lyn.

"How is she doing?" Brody stopped at the door, wanting to peak inside, but his instincts held him back.

Nigan sat inside, chanting. But when he saw Brody peaking in the door, he rose and walked to the doorway. "She has shifted back. It is only a matter of time and she will be like her old self."

"A feisty little she devil who is always taunting and teasing? I can't wait." Brody let out a deep belly laugh.

The scent of herbs filled the air surrounding them, the heat unbearable. Steam rose from the heated rocks inside the tent.

"When can we see her?" Sadie stood at Brody's side, her hand on his arm. He felt the tension and the fear, knew it could only be eliminated when Sadie saw Lyn healed.

"Now would be fine." Nigan stepped aside to let them enter.

"Lyn..." Sadie kneeled beside her. "I'm so sorry this happened. It was my fault. I should have never..."

"It wasn't." Lyn smiled at them. "Battle scars are good." She laughed but stopped, holding her hand on her ribs.

"Well, little sis, you proved yourself worthy. You fought the good fight, and I will eternally be grateful to you for saving my woman."

Sadie shot him an interesting glance. He laughed and pulled Sadie close to his side, reveling in her warmth and the seductive power she held over him. She was his woman for the moment, and he did mean to keep her. He would find a way to meet her in the middle.

"Thank you. Now you owe me big time," Lyn said. "And I will collect. You can be sure of that."

Brody stood and pulled Sadie to her feet. "Rest. You can collect later. Know we will return to torment you."

They stood outside the hut. "Brody, I'm not your woman. You've got to stop thinking that way. I'm leaving in less than a week, and I don't know if I'm ever going to see you again."

He roughed his hands through his hair. The last thing he needed was an argument with Sadie. The last thing he wanted was for her to leave him. But he knew he would have to let her go in order to get her back. The thought of life without his sweet sexy Sadie made his heart ache with longing.

Hand in hand they walked to the house. Inside, he pulled her close, her back against his chest. Closing his eyes, he let his hands rest on her abdomen. He felt the life inside her, a tiny being, theirs.

She would return. He had never meant for her to leave, carrying their child. But that one time they had not used protection. They had been so caught in passion the thought never crossed his mind.

"I understand." And he meant to do that, understand. "I'll help you with the rest of your notes. Then we can start back to town. I'm sure you want to return as soon as possible."

She slanted him a strange look. "Now you're rushing me home? It's me who doesn't grasp what you're saying."

"Princess, I want what you want—always will. Even if we don't see the same vision." The truth did not startle him. He meant every word.

She took his hand in hers. "Okay." She pulled him to their room. Rummaging through a stack of notebooks, she held up the one she wanted. Then stuck a pencil behind her ear. Lord, but she looked sexy, sitting on the rug in his room, legs crossed, hair disheveled thumbing through her notes.

"What do you want me to look for?" Brody accepted the spiral pad and sat down next to her.

"There is a map. I've traced the migration path of the monarch butterfly from Alaska to here. You'll find scribblings next to each set of data. I'm trying to match up what interviewees have told me."

He felt unsure but he followed her directions. Each time he thought he found something important, he'd show it to her. A few hours later they emerged, Sadie with a grin a mile wide.

"What happens now?"

"I go back to school and present this. Our team wants to receive grant money so we can work on this proposal. I have to present it to a board, and they will decide if it has merit."

"I could go with you." He looked to the horizon, praying she would allow him his way. God, but he'd miss this land. Yet he would follow her anywhere she travelled, even to a city.

"Why? You'd be lost and alone."

"You saying I wouldn't fit in?"

"Yup."

"Not smart enough for your doctoral candidates." His stomach rolled with worry and fear. Trepidation surged within.

"You're smarter."

~ * ~

Lyn floated in a surreal dream somewhere between the earth and the heavens above. A dark haired man with sharp rugged features faded in and out of her head, prowling the vacant spaces.

He sat down next to her and stared at her as if he knew her. But she'd never seen him before. The connection between them was strong and dangerous to her senses. She tried to reach out to him, but he moved away.

"Rest, little one, my Sugar." His voice soothed her and perhaps helped the healing process. She wasn't sure who he was or his mission here, but she liked him by her side. When he left her, she tried to call out to him, but found she had no voice.

"I'm resting," she tried to tell him, "come back to me. I need you by my side. You give me courage."

Lyn tried to reach out to him and take his hand to pull him back, but she didn't have the strength.

"The Chullachaqui is dead. He can hurt you no more." Sometime in her dreams, he returned. "That was foolish of you, to take on the Amazonian devil by yourself. In the future you must take more caution in your affairs."

"I'm capable. I did nothing foolish." She tried to explain to him and wondered at that. He was not her keeper, had no say in her life. But it seemed he cared about what she did.

"Of course, I didn't mean to imply you were not. But you were one against him."

"Sadie would be lost to us, if I had not stepped in and helped."

He grimaced, his brows furrowing. "This is true, but..."

"But what?"

"I can't say. In time you'll understand."

Chapter Ten

"She'll be back to Cactus Junction before you can blink." Carr danced, placing imaginary blows around Brody' chest and arms. After Sadie drove away, Carr and Brody travelled back to gramp's ranch. He felt closest to Sadie there and Carr insisted on accompanying him. They didn't take time to visit their family home.

"I blinked." Brody wasn't in the mood for his little brother's humor. He needed to be alone, to drown in his misery. His heart ached for the loss of Sadie. He knew he'd miss her, but he never understood how hard this would be. Time had a way of healing most wounds, but this time the loss was debilitating.

"Then go after her." In brotherly fashion Carr wrapped an arm around Brody's shoulder then stepped back. "The sooner the better, I always say. Don't waste the moment."

"She has to figure this out on her own." The truth slapped him in the face every time he thought it or said it. He couldn't force her to stay with him. She had her world and her ways as well as her dreams. The chance to fulfill her life was all she asked for. And he didn't want to give it to her. Space...

Space such an underrated word, but Sadie needed and wanted time away from him. So important for her to realize she would be happy with him not without him. He wondered if she knew she carried his child. What would she do when she discovered the truth?

The car and the dust vanished from view weeks ago. Go after her? She'd left and the loss stole his breath. Brody turned. The mountains loomed behind him. He also needed space—to think and adjust. Memories of Sadie in his arms haunted his soul.

"Where you goin'?"

Carr's voice hit him like a blow to the chest. His heart stopped then with a deep breath, it began to beat again. "Infinity Cliff." Brody knew this was the last place he should go, the memories there vivid.

"Good place to wallow in your broken dreams. Want company?" Carr seemed to guess the answer.

"That's what I plan on doin'. And no, company would ruin my self pity." Brody walked away with the heat of Carr's gaze warming his back. Self pity, wallow in broken dreams, no, he aimed to figure out how long he could give her before he chased after her and dragged her back to the mountains, to this life.

"Don't forget a change of clothes. Seeing you butt naked is not something I relish." Carr shouted from behind then Brody heard a deep belly laugh.

"Yeah, like when you carried Lyn home." Brody couldn't help the parting shot, and he longed for Carr to find his woman and leave him alone.

"I'm coming after you if you're not back by sunset."

The echo of Carr's words taunted him. Brody walked when he needed to run. At the moment he hung on to sanity by a thin thread. A fight would do him good. Briefly, he'd thought about taking his emptiness out on Carr. He'd changed his mind. Running into the Chullachaqui or his evil twin might relieve the tension building. But the devil was dead. And he prayed there was no evil twin.

The rocks where he meant to leave his clothes towered above. He stripped naked.

His calf muscles began to tingle with the increased blood flow, felt the sensation inch up his body, experienced the increase of adrenalin surge through his prepared body. He had just shifted into his cat form--a sleek black jaguar. Even in his human form, his cat never left him. It was always there, prowling around in his head. Chasing demons away was his intent. Although he knew, deep inside, this demon would only leave when he found his Sadie again.

The earth racing beneath his paws was nirvana to his soul. Wind against his face, heart pounding beneath his ribs, he needed to forget. Forgetting was impossible.

Seconds turned to minutes, his breath rasped out. Built for speed, not endurance, he needed to stop and catch his breath. But he ran. He ran until his mind shut down and his body collapsed.

Infinity Cliff in front, the sheer drop off inches away. He sat back on his haunches feeling tears form in eyes. In two short weeks his life had changed. Then two more weeks had passed. Time seemed to move on without him.

For good or bad, he had to find a way to bring Sadie back to mend his broken heart. He searched his mind but found emptiness. His tail switched with impatience and his claws scraped hard rock. All his senses finely honed and tuned into the environment.

Here earth and sky met, fire and water were as one, and the wind mourned a soulful wail. Eagles soared above on currents only they could see. He didn't know how long he watched the world turn. The sun rose in the sky then set. A moon hung on the horizon as darkness descended.

At one moment, he thought he caught her scent then that sensation vanished. He needed to hear her footsteps, but that was to no avail. To wrap his arms around her and hear her laughter would fill the dark hole that had been created upon her departure.

Giving her the space and time he knew she needed was the hardest thing he'd ever tried. When his mind cried out to him to race down the mountains to be by her side, it was all he could think about.

In his cat form, Carr appeared by his side. Brody felt a sense of relief, camaraderie only his brother could fill. Carr teased but he understood how his heart ached. And he'd told him he'd find him if he hadn't returned when the sun cast its shadow on the mountains.

One day Carr would find his mate. Brody prayed the journey would be easier than this one he embarked upon. But somehow he doubted it. The journey to find love was never easy.

Carr motioned with his head. He seemed to want Brody to follow him. They ran then wrestled together. One day turned to the next. Then with loping strides, they made their way down the mountain to the cave where Brody and Sadie had spent the night. It seemed such a long time ago.

The brothers sat on the edge of the hot springs where Brody had made love with his Sadie. It seemed he remembered every caress and every sound. The gentle flow of the water around their bodies was something he meant to feel again with his princess.

Brody shifted. Carr did the same. They both slipped into the water. The heat penetrated Brody's soar muscles. The pair had traveled miles, played, fought and listened to the whispers of the earth, wind and sky. He thought of the tiny life inside Sadie. Even though she didn't believe it or want it, she'd be a wonderful mother.

"Have you come to any decisions?" Carr sunk neck deep into the water, splashing the liquid with one hand.

"Time has passed. Days have turned into weeks. I miss her." Brody let water drip from his raised hand. *I miss her so damn much.*

"You're a love sick fool." Carr laughed then quieted for a moment. "I would not wish this malady on anyone."

A belly laugh from Brody followed. A weight had been lifted from his heart. "This is true."

"What are you going to do about it?"

Ignoring the question, Brody laughed again. "What I couldn't do a month ago. She has had her space. Now it is time I plead my case. Whether she wants to or not, she will have to make a decision soon."

"Your case being..."

"Marriage, if she will have me. A home in the Sierra Madres, if she will agree. In return I will follow her on all her expeditions. Hell, I'll live in the city if she'll agree to it."

"If not?"

"I won't return here but will stay by her side as close as she will allow. I will know my child."

Carr inhaled a sharp breath then air whistled through his teeth. "You knocked her up? She left here pregnant? Fuck, you didn't use protection? I'm shocked."

"We were careless—once." He let his head fall back on the ledge then closed his eyes, trying for long deep breaths.

"I'm left speechless."

"A new one for you." Brody splashed his brother.

Carr responded. The pair tussled in the water, ducking each other, coming up for air then repeating the process.

To Brody the fight released his soul, helped heal the scars Sadie had left him with. His mind raced with new details about the up coming months. He didn't want to surprise Sadie, but he didn't want to give her time to form excuses. The load lifted from his shoulders, he felt ready to pursue his dreams.

The pair leaned back, once again the water stilled. Silence surrounding them echoed throughout.

"I will leave in two weeks." Brody closed his eyes then opened them to look into Carr's grin. "There is no time for rest."

"Not when you have plans to make."

"I could use a night's sleep." Brody had spent little time in bed and the few hours there were not productive. Sleep had been elusive sense Sadie ran away.

"Then stay here."

"Good idea. I'll meet you at the ranch tomorrow." Brody didn't think Carr would agree even to give him a moment's peace. Yet, he appreciated his brothers concern.

"Not in this lifetime. I'm not leaving you to your own devices."

Brody stretched out and Carr followed suit. The sun would rise on several new days before he would return to town and his home. He had travelled two days to get here. Just as before with Sadie, he would take two days to return.

One more week and he could travel to the city. Carr would be prepared then to take over his duties in the village. For how long Brody couldn't say, but he would take as much time as needed. It might be years before he returned. But he would never come home without Sadie.

When the sun sunk behind the hills, he rose and nodded at Carr.

They made good time, seldom stopping to rest. Rain fell on the dusty side streets the day they arrived. Earlier, they stopped to shift back to human form and dress.

"It's about time the two of you came home. Where's Lyn?" Their mother stood in the kitchen, dough on her fingers. With her forearm, she pushed hair from her face.

"Lyn was hurt but she's going to be fine." Brody gave his mom a hug then a quick kiss to her cheek.

"Hurt? How? My children have been gone for so long and I've not heard one word."

"Defending Sadie against an Amazonian devil." Carr kissed his mom's cheek.

"Thought you knew." Brody grabbed an apple from the kitchen counter.

"Well, the pair of you haven't been home, and I guess you never heard of cell phones. No one's said a thing." She turned back to kneading the bread.

"Sorry, Mom, guess I had a lot on my mind." Brody bit into the apple. Juice slipped down one side. With the back of his hand, he wiped it away.

"That's no excuse as well you know." She pointed one finger at Brody.

"What about you, Carr? What's your excuse?"

"Sorry, mom. I don't have one. I just thought you all knew what happened."

"All right then, as long as she's going to be fine. I suppose she got herself into a fight with that demon and didn't fare so well. Just glad the pair of you came to her rescue.

"Mom, I'm leaving and I don't know when I'm coming home." Brody waited for his mom to object but the protest didn't come. The stunned look on his mom's face took a long time to vanish.

~ * ~

Tears ran down Sadie's cheeks as she drove away. Wiping them away with the back of her hand, she vowed she would not care for

Brody McKenna. He was too... He was too much for her. Too much man...

But he'd lodge himself in her soul and forgetting would be impossible. The memories would never leave, perhaps in time they'd diminish.

Hours later she pulled into her parking space at the apartment complex she rented. Tears continued to spill from her eyes. No amount of swearing and trying to think of other things besides Brody worked. Nothing made the image of him vanish.

At her door she fumbled for her keys, her backpack and bag falling to the floor while she searched for the means to unlock her door. A few seconds later, she was inside. Her cell in hand she called one of the research partners and set up a meeting. All five had returned and were ready to decide on a project to present to the panel.

She grabbed a package of chips then sat down with her laptop to write her proposal. Two bags of chips and a half hour later she finished. Sadie found a bottle of wine and poured herself a glass then wandered into the bathroom. A long hot soak might help wash the memories away.

But it wasn't to be. She found herself thinking of Brody and the hot springs. The way his touch felt. Her body responded with longing. More than anything she wanted him inside her. Needed the feel of belonging to him, listening to his laughter and the easy way he had of looking at life.

"God, this can't be happening." She wanted to shout out to the world. "I'm an independent woman. I don't need a man to complete me." But she needed Brody.

Heaving a long sigh, she closed her eyes and sipped on the wine. The merlot didn't even taste good. The water grew cold. She rose from the tub, drying herself and putting on an old terrycloth robe.

She settled in front of the TV hoping to find something to take her mind off the man she couldn't forget.

Sweet sexy Sadie...

Oh how she'd love to hear his voice. She reached for her cell, thinking of calling him, but put it back not wanting to give him false hope. She had things to accomplish. Pinning away for a man she'd just met was not on her agenda. Getting ready for tomorrow was imperative.

Weeks later, papers in hand, Sadie and her team sat in front of a panel, waiting to find out if their project would be approved. It had taken the team longer than usual to decide on the proposal. They didn't choose the Sierra Madres and Sadie's project. Once again they were headed south to the Amazon. Sadie wasn't sure she'd go with them. Ever present in her mind was the image of the Chullachaqui.

But she wanted the best for her team, and she would support them at all cost. Her nerves frayed and her heart accelerated. She inhaled a long deep breath. So much depended on this meeting. Tapping her fingernails on the armrest of her chair, she searched the faces of the men and women in front of her for some clue.

One of the men cleared his throat. "I'm sorry to say none of this can be funded. It's not because we don't like the proposal. You are a week too late. All of the grant money has been handed out. So..."

"You will have to wait for another year. You can present this or something new next year." A woman finished the sentence.

"Another year?" The five teammates echoed.

Another year...

Sadie felt numb, an emptiness invading her soul and weighting her down. She had given up so much to get to this point, and now because of timing, her dreams would be put on hold. This couldn't be happening.

Outside the old brick building where her dreams had toppled one of the team members suggested. "Coffee...?"

They started for the restaurant. Sadie looked up, her breath caught in her throat. Across the street she caught sight of a man. "No... Oh, my..." *Fuck...*

He leaned against a lamppost and seemed to be watching her. Swallowing the lump in her throat, "I'll meet up with you guys later." She'd never expected this, never thought Brody would come down from his mountain paradise. But there he was—just as handsome and seemingly devil-may-care as he always was.

"What is it?"

"Something I have to take care of before I can make plans." The walk sign came on and she started across the street. Brody stood straight, his hands at his sides, his expression unreadable.

"Sadie?" A tremor in his voice surprised her.

"What are you doing here?" She pulled her hair back from her face. "I didn't think I'd ever see you again."

"If you can't stay in the mountains, I've decided I'd come to you." He stepped toward arms outstretched. "If you'll have me."

"I-I, you'll wither and die here. I never asked—or expected you to do this for me."

"For us and I won't fade away. Not as long as you are with me." Brody stroked her cheek, a sad smile on his face.

The simple gesture sent goose bumps spiraling through her body. "I'm barely in my apartment. It's small and there's nowhere for you to run—no trails—just concrete. I didn't plan... There are things you don't know about me." Guilt swept through her. He'd told and shown her everything. He had no secrets. But she had not trusted him enough to tell him about her mother and father. Oh, she'd told him they weren't good parents but not the real truth. He'd run from her if he knew. Genetics don't lie. She most likely acted just like her mother.

"I promise I won't get in your way. You won't even know I'm there." His promise was not plausible. They'd be in bed every waking and sleeping hour if he lived in her apartment.

Sadie didn't know what to say. She was so happy to see him. Tears formed in her eyes. "You don't belong in the city."

He touched a lone teardrop. "Don't cry."

Telling Brody they were tears of joy and loneliness as well crossed her mind. But she didn't want to give him hope where there was none. And if she encouraged him in any way...

"Give me a chance—us a chance." Brody rested his hand at the base of her neck.

A second chance at happiness seemed little to ask. She wanted it too--happiness. For a moment she looked at the sidewalk then back into his vivid green eyes. "Okay."

His grin stretched wide across his handsome face. "It's all good, princess. I'll make sure of it."

"I know you will."

"You won't regret this."

"Our research project wasn't approved. We were too late. The grant money was given out to other teams." She didn't know why, but the research didn't seem as important. "They wanted to go back to the Amazon. I don't think I could do that. The thought terrifies me."

"I'm sorry, truly."

"You would not wish failure for me. I know that." She placed her hand in his. "Come on, I want you to meet my team. We're having coffee."

"I would like that. I want to know all your friends. I want to know everything about you."

Hours later they'd had coffee, dinner and a few laughs. Now Sadie fumbled with her key, trying to unlock the door. Her fingers were all thumbs. But she wanted him so much she shook with the need.

"Brody..."

"Here." He took the keys from her. The door opened. Brody swept her into his arms then kicked the door shut behind them after he stepped into the room. "Where's the bed?"

"That way." She pointed down the hall while she ran her fingers through his hair. *What will I do without him in my life? How have I survived these last weeks?*

"I've missed you so damn much." His mouth found hers, lips teeth tongue danced together. He set her down.

"Me too." She slipped her hands under his t-shirt, moving it up, her fingers touching his abs then his chest.

He placed her on the bed before lifting his arms for her to take it off. "God, Sadie, my sweet sexy Sadie. How I've missed you." He fumbled with the buttons on her shirt, ripping part of the cloth in his haste.

"Let me." Her breath rushed out with pent up desire.

"It's been too damn long." He slipped off the rest of his clothes. Sadie did the same.

The sex was over in seconds. She lay for a minute, replete, trembling, the emptiness vanishing. Then his hands began another gentle exploration of her body. Touching every part of her, lingering at her nipples, tracing her lips then giving his attention to her clit.

"Again?" She didn't need the answer to that question, his cock was hard and pulsing against her stomach.

"Again." His raspy voice sent her heart racing with need. His mouth gave attention to one nipple. She arched her back, in a silent plea for more. He obliged.

Deep inside her, she didn't care how fast he was, or how many times. She would make love with him every time he wanted. For Sadie the sex was no longer the best sex of her life but it was making love.

And she'd never realized it before. With Brody it had always been love. At first she hadn't understood the difference.

Later, they lay in each other's arms. His sweat sheened body entranced her. The muscles relaxed now but if she touched him, they seemed to move.

"We have to talk." The baby, their baby grew inside her womb. He deserved to know, but she hadn't been able to call him and tell him over the phone. And she hadn't had the time to drive to the Sierra Madres. Maternal feelings still so knew to her, she'd needed space to figure things out. Now everything was clear. She knew what she had to do.

Brody sat up then leaned against the headboard. His abs rippled with the movement. She wanted to touch him again.

Enough is enough, Sadie girl.

"About what?" His question reverberated around the room then settled in her gut. He was her baby's daddy. How would he react? Would he be pleased or horrified?

She sat up, pulling covers around her then played with the material of the comforter. "I—"

"You're nervous. Don't be. You can tell me anything."

"This has repercussions I'm not sure I'm mature enough to deal with." She leaned back, letting her head ease against the wall. With her eyes closed, she tried deep even breaths. But nothing calmed her rolling tummy.

"It's always easiest to spit it out." His fingers closed around hers, separating her from the security of the fabric. He lifted her hand and kissed the palm.

"Okay." She opened her eyes and faced the man she loved. "I'm pregnant." Sadie swallowed hard, waiting for his reply.

His grin lit up the room. "That wasn't so hard. Was it?"

"Damn hard."

He laughed a full belly laugh then leaned over and kissed her. "How do you feel about it?"

"Now you look nervous." She pushed back the fear and the excitement. Lord, but this was the first time she'd felt pleasure when she'd thought about the baby.

"I am. I admit it. Nervous. I want to be the best baby daddy ever."

Sadie poked him in the chest, a strange feeling coming over her. "Did you know?"

"That last time I saw you and I held you in my arms I felt the life beneath my fingertips. Yes, but I knew you would need to come to terms with this on your own. You didn't need me hovering over you."

"You are a wise man, Brody McKenna."

"Now, what are you—we going to do?" His lips thinned and one eyebrow arched.

"We?"

"I am the father."

"Yes, but I never thought..."

"That I could or should have a say about this child that is both of ours?" He wasn't smiling.

"Of course you should. But I was so wrapped up in everything that was going on, I could only think about my feelings."

"And those are..." Brody drummed his fingers on the bed.

"If you were in your cat form, your tail would be swishing back and forth." She almost laughed at the image that brought to her mind.

"I'm not." His voice was harder than she'd expected.

Guess it was time to tell him. "At first I was going to get an abortion." She heard him suck air. "Then I knew I couldn't do that. The baby was conceived in love. So I considered adoption, but knew if I gave my child away, I would never stop looking for the babe."

"So you have decided to have our child." His voice rang of impatience.

"I want more than that." She paused, trying to form the words that would change her life forever. "Brody, I love you. I think I always have. I was too stubborn to admit it. But you should know, my mother left my father. He waited for her but she never came back to him. I don't want that to happen with us. He grieved for her so much, he was never a father to me."

Without a moment's notice, he pulled her into his arms. She clung to him as if he were her lifeline. "God, I thought I would never hear those words. I think I've loved you since the first day I saw you, butt in the air, trying to revive your dehydrated car. You won't be like your mother. Sadie, why are you crying?"

She sniffed then reached for a tissue. "Tears of joy."

He touched the drop on her cheek, kissed her then ran his fingers along her spine. She arched into him. A few minutes later he was deep inside her and she shuddered with the force of her climax while his seed filled her.

"We have to stop meeting this way." Sadie pushed back then brushed a lock of hair from his eyes.

"No, we don't." Out of bed, he tugged on her hand. "Let's go celebrate. I'm sure there is a bar or two still open. I want to buy you a glass of champagne."

"It's so late. And I can't have alcohol." She followed him and he tossed her the clothes she'd shed before their lovemaking.

"It's not--late. And I didn't think about that. We've got a lifetime to live together, and I intend to start living it right now."

Dressed and walking hand in hand down the boulevard near her apartment, they stopped at a bar. He ordered one glasses of champagne and one of sparkling grape juice. She wanted artichoke dip and chips. The sound system played hits from the eighties.

"There are a lot of new things to think about." She munched on a dip filled chip.

"Like what?"

"Food, rest, baby things, cribs, diapers, car seats." The list seemed endless.

"Since we put the cart in front of the horse, let's make things right." Brody rose from his seat and on one bended knee, he reached into his pocket and brought out a small black box.

Sadie's tears flowed again. She wasn't positive but...

He opened it and held it out to her. On black velvet sat the most gorgeous and gigantic diamond she'd ever seen.

"Will you marry me?"

"I—I." She didn't want to hesitate, but she hadn't expected this—a proposal.

Brody stayed on one knee, looking so patient and kind. His hand clenched the little box. He looked expectant. Then he cocked his head.

She inhaled a long fortifying breath. "Yes..."

He closed his eyes then opened them, a look of relief then a smile. "I thought for a moment you were going to say no. My heart hammers in my chest."

"Brody, I love you and this is what I want. I never thought marriage was for me, and I'm still afraid I'll botch it all up."

"Like your parents?"

"They were horrible to each other and..."

He took the ring out and slipped it on her finger. "You are a beautiful person, inside and out. You will be a wonderful wife and mother."

Epilogue

Two Years Later

"Do you think he's going to be a shifter? I never quite bought that stuff about it only takes one gene." Sadie twirled a dandelion between two fingers while she watched her son play in the sandbox.

"Does it matter? But I do think he will be a fighter as his name implies." Brody knew in his heart Sadie wouldn't care. But she'd ignored the topic. He didn't know what she thought.

"I don't know the first thing about raising a child let alone a baby who can change forms." She pointed at the child. "Look at him so carefree and fun loving. I want to give him the world."

"From my point of view we've done a fabulous job." He knew he patted himself on the back, but he'd always known he'd be a great parent. Of course the challenging years were still to come.

"He's happy and healthy and I love him so much." Sadie leaned back, slanting her head to the sky, feeling the heat of the sun against her face.

"Mommy, play with me."

"Come here." Brody motioned for the boy. On tiny little legs, he ran to his father and jumped. The pair rolled backwards, tumbling against the ground, Brody lifting him high into the air.

He giggled, "Tickle me Daddy."

Brody complied, tickling him and laughing all the while. They wrestled on the grass for a few minutes before Brody sat up.

"Look at me, I practice'."

The boy suddenly started shaking and twitching.

"Sloane!" Sadie cried out.

"It's okay, he's shifting."

"Except that one time, I've never seen you do it. And when you first started shifting, you shocked me so much I couldn't breathe."

"He's a child and curious. He must have felt the urge when he was alone and experimented. Yeah, you fell over the cliff." Brody beamed, feelings of pride for his son swept through him.

The boy had shifted and now he sat on his haunches, tail twitching, head cocked to one side. His tattered clothing lay in a tiny heap beside him. He bounded to Sadie and into her lap. Sadie laughed and scratched behind his ears.

"Now, I don't know what your father plans, but you have only have one change of clothes in the diaper bag and a couple of diapers. So you are going to need to be careful." Sadie paused then turning to Brody, "Does he understand any of this?"

"It's all instinctual. He doesn't need to understand yet. He doesn't know he is different. In this clan you are the unique one. He will soon see his father and aunts and uncles shift." Brody reached out a hand to caress his son.

The boy leapt from his mama's lap and raced across the lawn turning in circles, stopping then pouncing on some imaginary creature. A few minutes later he shifted back.

Naked he walked to his father who had already pulled a second set of clothing from the bag as well as a diaper.

The boy let his father diaper and dress him. "I'm a proud papa."

The boy beamed and giggled delightedly. "I do again?"

"No. You must take your clothes off before you shift. Your mama's afraid you might run out of clothing."

"Me hungry," he said. "Want grapes."

"Me too." Brody set out a lunch of finger foods for his son then turned his attention to the meal his mother had made for them.

"How many children do you want?" Sadie licked the icing off her fingers.

"At least two more." Brody knew it was time to tell Sadie as of three nights ago she now carried twins. But he wasn't sure how she would take the news. Women liked to tell their men when they were pregnant not the other way around.

"So..." She cocked her head to one side and stared pointedly at him. "Is there something you're not telling me?"

"Well..." Now that she'd pressed him, he fumbled for the words.

"Don't you dare lie to me, Brody McKenna."

"Twins. You will have twins in about nine months."

"When were you going to tell me?" She poked him in the chest. "When I was waddling along behind you? I'm telling you right now, I'm not going to be known as a barefoot and pregnant wife."

"I wasn't. I meant to let you tell me, but you have this way of making me tell you everything. I can't keep secrets and well you know. You will be known, Sadie McKenna as whatever you want to be known as. You are now as you were before--an independent and strong woman."

"Are you happy?"

"Of course but I think the main question is, are you happy? You didn't want children."

"I'm the happiest, proudest parent in the universe. I love you so much."

"My sweet sexy Sadie, I love you more."

About the Author
achristay@aol.com

Born in Medford, Oregon, novelist Christine Young has lived in Oregon all of her life. After graduating from Oregon State University with a BS in science, she spent another year at Southern Oregon State University working on her teaching certificate, and a few years later received her Master's degree in secondary education and counseling. Now the long, hot days of summer provide the perfect setting for creating romance. She sold her first book, Dakota's Bride, the summer of 1998 and her second book, My Angel to Kensington. Her teaching and writing careers have intertwined with raising three children. Christine's newest venture is the creation of Rogue Phoenix Press. Christine is the founder, editor and co-owner with her husband. They live in Salem, Oregon.

Other books by Christine Young
Available at Rogue Phoenix Press

Catching Meara
The first book in the McKenna Clan Series

Meara Thorton was a feisty, world-class computer hacker—cornered by the FBI and shockingly given the chance to be their newly acquired technical analyst. Brilliant and intuitive, yet aching with the loss of everyone she has cared about, her restless heart led her to discover a love she fought and a world she didn't know could possibly exist.

Jace McKenna was an enigma, a loner, impossibly handsome, sincere and committed. The Apache shapeshifter blood running through his veins burned hotter than the blistering Sierra Madre sun. Jace knew the moment he caught Meara's scent she was his for eternity.

Highland Honor
The first book in the Highland Series

Willfully stubborn, innocently courageous, Callie Whitcomb braves a journey through the treacherous highlands to the Macpherson castle. Callie flees from an unwanted marriage as well as her ruthless half brother. Naively she believes Colin MacPherson, the head of the clan, is loyal to her father and will give her sanctuary, protecting her from the vile plans that have been made for her.

As hard and as unyielding as the winter storms that sweep through the countryside, Colin is irresistibly drawn to the impetuous beauty who has magically appeared on his doorsteps. Despite his vows of revenge against her father, she stirs his passion as well as his sense of justice...but to love her would violate all his vows of revenge.

Highland Magic
The second book in the Highland Series

Throughout the Highlands she is known as Keely, the witch woman. She is a great healer-a woman whose dreams come true. Ian MacPherson is a man who puts honor, loyalty and duty above everything. Their lives are entwined when Ian is sent by the Scottish King to bring Keely to trial for witchcraft. He is attacked and left for dead, but Keely rescues him. When he wakes, he discovers he has no memory. As he remembers his lost past, Ian finds that his need to protect the woman who has saved his life eclipses his duty to his king and country., He is a man torn between honor and duty to his country and the woman he loves.

Highland Song
The third book in the Highland Series

With her white-gold hair and azure eyes, Lainie MacPherson is as wild and untamed as the rugged Scottish Highlands where she was raised. Lainie vowed to avenge her rape. Recklessly, she defies English laws and the man who raped her puts a bounty on her head. The man who is sent to bring her to Edinburgh sets a dangerous trap. With nothing left to live for the beautiful Scottish spy steals the sealed documents the English soldier has tempted her with.

When the exquisite temptress takes the bait and runs off with not only the forged documents but the purses of the men in the tavern, Aaron Slade vows to hunt her down and bring her to justice, never dreaming she will tame his jaded soul. When Aaron discovers the truth about the tempestuous woman who stirs his passion to the point of madness, he dares not love her, but desires her with all his soul.

Dakota's Bride
The first book in the Lakota/Pinkerton Series

When Emma St. John received her brother's letter imploring her to escape her stepfather's vengeful scheme and to trust Dakota Barringer with her life, she was willing to chance it. But the handsome, brooding riverboat owner Emma found in Natchez a danger of another kind. For Emma soon found herself surrendering to an unrelenting desire.

Raised by the Sioux when his parents were killed, Dakota had been betrayed once before by a white woman. He wasn't about to trust another, especially one claiming that her stepfather, a powerful U.S. senator, had framed her as a murderess. But he couldn't let Emma's intoxicating effect on him. Now Dakota would risk his very life to protect the innocent beauty who had seduced him with her tender love.

My Angel
The second book in the Lakota/Pinkerton Series

A BEAUTY IN BUCKSKINS

When her father decided to send her to a finishing school back East, Angela Chamberlain refused to be confined to stuffy drawing rooms. Instead, the daring spitfire who could shoot like a man and ride like the wind longed for a life of adventure and romance—and she knew exactly who could give it to her. Devil Blackmoor was a hired gun with a dangerous reputation. But Angela was willing to go to the ends of the earth to capture the handsome devil's heart.

A DEVIL IN DISGUISE

He'd come to America looking for excitement, but Devil Blackmoor got more than he bargained for when he encountered a beautiful rebel who answered his kisses with a wild innocence that touched his very soul. Yet standing between them were more obstacles than either ever dreamed. For Devil had strapped on a gun for the wrong man. And that made Angela his enemy. Now he'll have to choose between his duty and the woman he loves more than life.

The Locket
The third book in the Lakota/Pinkerton Series

The year is 1894. Seeking revenge for crimes against his family, Misha Petrovich follows a path that leads straight to Ariel Cameron's boarding house in Mist Harbor, Oregon. A family heirloom in Ariel's possession leads Misha to believe she is guilty. The locket has been handed down to the oldest girl in the Petrovich family for generations. Ariel is innocent of wrong doing, but her father is not. Misha is torn by his feelings for Ariel and his need for restitution against her father. Knowing that the relationship between them is fragile, Misha does everything in his power to protect Ariel's father. His efforts are to no avail when her father is shot. Ariel comes to realize Misha's steadfast courage and determination to protect her and her father despite what has happened to his family. Ariel's love and devotion heals Misha's heart.

The Talisman
The fourth book in the Lakota/Pinkerton Series

Running from a marriage that lasted one night, Dr. Moriah McKeown discovers the land she has settled on is coveted by determined and lawless men. Yet the proud young woman who once vowed never to abandon her home has second thoughts when her adopted children are threatened. Her only recourse is to enlist the aid of a dark, dangerous gun for hire.

Haunted by the past and a betrayal he will never forgive, Ian Civanovich uses his fast gun and his reckless courage to forget the faithlessness of a woman in his past. He will trust no female--nor will he rest until the threat hovering over Moriah McKeown is put to rest.

Forever His
The fifth book in the Lakota/Pinkerton Series

Struggling to come to terms with the part she played in Jacob St. John's death, Etta Barringer resigns from Pinkerton Agency and seeks peace and solace in a Rocky Mountain Cabin.

Jacob has vowed to discover the reason Etta has betrayed him, sold him out to his enemy and left him for dead.
Isolated in their cabin, they discover their love for each other and learn to trust. But the trust is shattered when Jacob learns she is married to his sworn enemy; the man who left him in the desert to die.

Allura
The first book in the Twelve Dancing Princesses Series

Allura McClellan is horrified by her father's decision to take out an ad in the Times awarding her to the man strong enough and smart enough to win her hand and uncover her secrets. She's an intelligent young woman who takes great delight in the freedom allotted to her by her father. She's well aware that marriage would effectively curtail the adventures she's shared with her sisters and cousins.

Hunter Gray is nothing like the other men who've arrived to vie for Allura's hand in marriage and everything that goes along with it. However, he is the first to refuse to concede defeat and pursue her despite her attempts to disguise her true appearance. It's her temperament that is of more concern to him than her looks. Hunter has worked all his life with the hope of someday owning his own land. Now that it looks like there's a very real possibility that everything he's ever wanted is within reach nothing is going to deter him – including Miss Allura's disagreeable disposition.

The Wager
The second book in the Twelve Dancing Princesses Series

Amorica Hepburn was sent to London to find a husband. Finding a man was the last item on her agenda. With her two cousins, Amorica wagers she can dissuade her suitor before the others. Despite her efforts she discovers a chemistry that cannot be denied. Suddenly she is the arrogant man's wife, pledged to a marriage neither desire. But swept off to his ancestral home above the Dover cliffs and into his strong embrace, Amorica is soon possessed by a raging passion for the husband she had vowed to despise…

Damian Andrews couldn't afford to trust the emerald-eyed spitfire who happened upon his secret. Amorica's hatred of all men of his kind only inflames the war that rages between them. Still, he can not control the intense desire his stubborn bride inspires, or make her surrender to his will until he has conquered the headstrong beauty on the battlefield of love…

A Marriage of Inconvenience
The third book in the Twelve Dancing Princesses Series

A REGAL BEAUTY

When the duchess decides to wed her to a wastrel and a fop, Ravyn Grahm takes matters into her own hands and declares her engagement to another man. Instead of fessing up and telling her great aunt what she has done, she goes through with the pretense. Aric Lakeland is the bastard son of an earl and has a dangerous reputation. But Ravyn is willing to do most anything to keep the duchess from discovering the lie.

A DEVIL-MAY-CARE SMUGGLER

He'd bought land in America, looking to put down roots and end his life of adventure, but Aric Lakeland got more than he bargained for when he encountered a beautiful heiress who made a promise she didn't want to keep. But the promise could not be undone and standing between them were more obstacles than either ever dreamed. Aric had made plans to spend the rest of his life in America and that was at odds with Ravyn's plan of living in England and running her father's estate. Now, he'll have to choose between his dreams and the woman he loves more than life.

Rebel Heart

HER REBEL SPIRIT DEFIED HIS OUTSIDERS SOUL...

She was velvet and silk, eyes the color of a summer storm and amber hair. Victoria DeMontville, because of a promise and a codicil to her father's will, was forced to marry one man to protect her from another. She hated Cameron Savage with a fierce passion. But to hold on to her genetic research and find a cure for the deadly Signe virus, she must pretend to love the enemy at her door, come with weapons of fire to melt her icy heart...

HIS OUTSIDERS TOUCH IGNITED RAGING PASSIONS...

He wore a mask, disguised as the Phantom, a true legend come to life. Even as war and debate over new genetic research engulfed them all, he would find his greatest adversary in the beauty who'd branded him an outsider and barbarian, the woman he was born to possess, his soul mate.

A St. Patrick's Day Tale
by
Christine Young, C. L. Kraemer, Genene Valleau

Tumble through time…

…to Ireland in 1817, when tensions are high between Protestants and Chatolics and faey people guide the fate of villagers. A lovely Catholic lass stumbles upon the weakly ritual fisticuffing between Irish lads. She falls into the lap of a handsome young Protestant. Family ties, grudges, and two conniving faeries threaten their budding love. But the faeries outsmart themselves when they hijack a time machine that has mysteriously appeared in their forest and are whisked to…

…Eugene, Oregon in the 20th century, amid a property feud between the local faeries and night elves. The conniving faeries from Olde Ireland try to stir up more mischief. However, a warrior gnome convinces the magic folk to control their own destiny, and forces the intruding faeries to take refuge in the time machine again, spinning their way toward…

…A modern day castle in western Oregon. An eccentric inventor is determined to reclaim his wayward time machine and save his beloved wife from her latest misadventure. If only they can travel safely past the black hole…

A Valentine's Anthology

The Lending Library-a fantasy by Christie L. Kraemer

Faeries try to fit into the human world when the forest where they make their home is destroyed by a mysterious enemy.

Chasing Rainbows-a contemporary romance by Genene Valleau

An eccentric aunt, an inventive uncle, a mother who wears poodle skirts, and a brother who wears pearls provide a hilarious backdrop for the courtship of a young woman who yearns for a "normal" family.

The Gift-an historical romance by Christine Young

A man and a woman on opposite sides of the Civil War get a second chance at love after one final battle returns soldiers to their war-torn homes to rebuild their lives.

Writing as AnnChristine
Safari Moon

Solo St. John, a wildlife photographer, is preparing for a trip to Alaska. Suddenly, Solo finds women of all sorts invading his privacy, his home and his office, all cooing nonsense words and blatantly throwing themselves at him. Solo doesn't know why, and he has no idea how to rid himself of the persistent women. He finally decides to beg a favor of his best buddy Nyssa Harrington.

In love with Solo for the past ten years and knowing he doesn't return her feelings Nyssa doesn't want to talk to Solo. She knows if she accepts his phone call, she will not be able to resist the temptation to hope again.

A Valentine's Anthology

Sharks
byAnnChristine

Will Lily and Jacob, best friends forever, find love or will they discover friendship is not enough for a relationship to take the final step into marriage.

The House on Berkley Street
by K. J. Dahlen

When Serenity is asked to find the truth in a forty-year old tragedy, someone in the town of White Oak, Texas doesn't want the truth told. Can they stop her before she finds out what they have kept hidden for so long?

The Placebo Effect
by Solstice Stevens

First, there was the poison. Then, there was a four story jump and the basketball hoop. Jessamyn Hamhill's life has been one validation attempt after another . . . until now.